Raven's Call

By
Mary Lee Peck

Reading Research Institute
Westerville, Ohio

Mary Lee Peck earned her Ph.D. in Education from The Ohio State University. She has taught at all levels from preschool to graduate school. She is the author of **The Mansion** and **Breakfast With Friends** and will soon release the sequel to Raven's Call. She has also authored several children's books and a college textbook in reading instruction.

Published by Reading Research Institute, Westerville, Ohio

ISBN 10: 1-931365-13-x
ISBN 13: 978-1-931365-13-0
Library of Congress Control Number: 2011923168

Front Cover image was purchased from iStock.com

This book is dedicated to my husband and sister who support me by listening to my stories and making suggestions; to my grandchildren who love horses and other animals; and to my brother-in-law who suggested the title for the book.

Chapter 1

"You were amazing tonight as always," shouted Roger trying to be heard above the deafening noise of the band and the screaming audience. "Listen to that applause. Your fans sure love you."

"Thanks," muttered Jan. "Now you need to get me out of here. We have a six-hour drive ahead of us to Oklahoma City. I want to get there early, so I can spend as much time as possible with my family before I have to leave again. Where's the motor coach?"

"It's just outside the stage door, but it's already surrounded by fans expecting autographs. You can't just breeze through there without at least signing a few."

Jan drew in a deep breath and slowly exhaled. "OK, but just a few. I really am exhausted. I didn't think I was going to get through that last set. I'm truly beat."

Roger was a savvy agent and was always protecting her image, but her first road trip as a star was grueling—not to mention expensive. She was physically exhausted from the back-to-back shows and was emotionally drained from worrying about the huge loan she had taken out for her share of the expenses to fund the tour. Although, with Roger's extensive connections in Nashville, she was one of the few overnight success stories in country music, the royalties she had earned from her first single and her album were not enough to pay the expenses of hauling a band, back-up singers, road crew, and equipment across ten states.

Roger had set up several generous sponsors for the tour, but even with their help, she had to provide some of the funding. She knew that a road tour was an essential part of a budding star's career, and she was thrilled when Roger first mentioned it. Touring as the feature act was the dream of her naïve ego. Now, even though the tour was pushing her new album straight to the top of *Billboard's* Hot Country Albums chart, and resulted in a cover photo of her on *People Magazine*, she wasn't sure that all of the excitement and recognition were worth it. For the glory, she had given away her privacy, her freedom, and the closeness that she loved with her family and their Texas ranch. Now she had others who depended on her for their financial well-being, and she had a whopping debt that would probably wipe out all her earnings from her new album. She sighed and tried to push the negative thoughts from her mind and to concentrate on just getting to the American Quarter Horse Association World Show in Oklahoma where she could be with her family and Raven, her majestic black stallion.

She definitely felt the effects of the road tour this time more than she had in previous trips as an opening act for several other country greats. Thank goodness, there were only three more stops after the World Show—just three more concerts and she would be able to go back to Texas for a few months. She missed being home, and she longed for the companionship of her two sisters, her young niece, and her handsome nephew. She missed riding and being around the horses. Even though she would be performing at the horse show, she would also be riding and connecting with her family and Raven, if only for a few days.

Roger and three security guards surrounded her as they exited through the stage door. Outside, additional security personnel kept her fans restrained behind sturdy ropes in an effort to keep an open pathway to her awaiting motor coach. The noise from their screaming and shouting was deafening, and their pushing and shoving were a little unnerving.

Scanning the crowd, Jan spotted a young girl buffeted around by the excited fans, and she reached out to take the autograph book that the child was holding. The girl was much younger than most of the fans and was trying desperately to avoid being shoved aside by the others who were pushing her from behind. Jan lifted the rope to let the little girl inside the protected area and leaned over to ask her name.

"Melanie," the young girl shouted trying to make herself heard above the screams of the other fans. "My name is Melanie Kirby but, please, make the autograph to Jamie. She's my older sister. She's very sick and in the hospital. We're both big fans."

"I'm sorry to hear about your sister," said Jan. "Hopefully, she'll get better soon." She felt her heart sink as the young girl glanced up at her with pools of tears gathering in her eyes and threatening to stream down her cheeks. "Where are your parents?" Jan asked, concerned that such a young child was alone in such a wild crowd of people.

"My dad brought me down here. He's waiting over there." Melanie pointed to a beat-up old van parked across the street. "My mom is with my sister. We didn't have enough money for tickets to the concert, but I wanted to get your autograph for Jamie."

Jan signed the autograph book, and then she took off her expensive hat and signed the brim. She placed the hat on the little girl's head, and the crowd went nuts applauding and shouting. On cue, Roger handed Melanie two albums and helped her through the crowd to the safety of her father's parked van. Jan continued to sign autographs until he got back.

"Sorry folks, that's all," Roger shouted waving his hands above his head. "Jan has to get on the road, so she can get to Oklahoma City in time for her next performance. Thanks for your support," he yelled as he tossed CDs to the crowd. "We love you!"

The security guards strained to hold back the shoving fans. Jan waved to them as Roger ushered her into the coach.

"Oh, my gosh," she groaned as she plopped down on the sofa inside of the motor coach. "I thought I was going to burst out crying when that little girl told me about her sister. Her sister's name is Jamie. What a coincidence, huh? Did you happen to get her address? I'd like to follow up with a note or something."

"Her father was waiting for her outside of the van when I got her through the crowd," answered Roger. "He must have thanked me a million times for the hat. That was a wonderful thing you did— expensive but thoughtful. I did get their name and address. Knowing you the way I do, I suspected that you'd want to follow-up with a personal card or something."

"Thanks. I want to find out more about her and her sister. I just kept thinking about my niece Jamie. I can't wait to get to the horse show, so I can give her a big hug. I don't know what I would do if something ever happened to her."

"Quit worrying. I'm sure she's fine. You're so sensitive when it comes to your family and the plight of others. It's that genuine compassion and insight that make your music touch the heart and souls of your fans." He squeezed her shoulder and then walked up to the front of the rig to talk with her driver, Bill Cranson. "Okay, Bill," he said opening the door that sealed the driver's compartment off from the rest of the coach. "Get us out of here. Take us back to the hotel first." Glancing back at Jan, he asked, "I'm assuming that you want to get a shower and change in the hotel before heading for Oklahoma, right?"

"Thanks, Roger," said Jan. "You think of everything. I really do appreciate you."

"That's my job, but it's a whole lot more fun when I know I'm appreciated." He sat back down beside her on the sofa and put his arm around her pulling her closer. She let her head fall against his shoulder. "Man, you *are* tired. This break comes at just the right time. And, please, stop worrying about the money for the tour. Every show is sold out, and your albums are flying out of the stores. You'll be able pay off the loan with no sweat."

Jan smiled up at him as their rig pulled away from the curb. She wished she could muster up just a little of his confidence. Through the heavily tinted windows of the motor coach, she could see the fans waving signs and breaking through the rope barrier trying to get closer to the coach. She did love singing to them, but she hated that she didn't actually know them. "There must be a thousand stories in that crowd, and I don't know any of them," she said closing her eyes and resting her head against Roger's broad, sturdy shoulder.

The trip to the hotel was a short one. With Roger leading the way, Jan quickly slipped out of the coach and into the back door of the hotel to avoid the throng of fans gathered around its entrance. She was aware of the stares from the people working in the kitchen as she hurried past them. She guessed she would never get accustomed to people staring at her and whispering *'that's her'* when she walked by.

She certainly didn't feel that she was anything

remarkable. She was just a cowgirl from Texas who happened to be born with a gift for music—something she had inherited from her dad. Although she loved music and entertaining, she disliked the whole hubbub that went with it. Whenever she went out now, she had to wear a wig and enormous sunglasses, so she could enjoy the sights or just go shopping. She would be glad to get back home to her ranch located between Fredericksburg and Luckenbach, Texas—the small Texas town made famous by Whalen Jennings and Willie Nelson. Back home she wasn't a big deal. People there had known her since she was born. They treated her just the same as anyone else, and it would be a welcomed relief to be real again.

"You do remember that I'm not going with you on the coach, right?" said Roger once they were inside the hotel room. "I'll arrive the day before the show, but you're on your own until then. Will you be Ok? I worry about not sending some security with you."

"I'm a big girl, Roger. I'm sure I'll be just fine, but I wish you would come. You love this horse show as much as I do."

"I can't hang around there, and you know why. I just can't be around Beth without actually wanting to be *with* her. You know that," he said. "She hates me and made it perfectly clear that she never wants to see me again. Unfortunately, I can't make myself feel the same way about her."

"But, that was almost two years ago," Jan pleaded. "You haven't had a drink in months, and you never even look at another woman."

"I'm sure she'll never give me another chance. I've tried twice since we broke it off," Roger lamented. "I hurt her too much." Then eager to change the subject, he said, "You'd better hurry if you want to get there early tomorrow morning."

Jan quickly showered and changed into comfortable jeans and her favorite baggy, old shirt before returning to the bus. Bill was standing outside of the coach talking to some curious onlookers when they came out the back door. Jan slipped past them while Roger issued some orders to Bill.

"Getting to Oklahoma City before morning is not as important as getting there safely," Roger reminded him. "So don't even think twice about stopping if you get the least bit sleepy."

Bill was an excellent driver, and Roger had made sure that he had plenty of rest earlier in the day. Jan wasn't the least bit worried about his driving. "We'll be okay, Roger. Quit hovering and let us get on the road," she joked throwing him a kiss. "I'll see you in a couple of days."

"I'll take good care of her," promised Bill.

Jan waved to Roger from inside of the coach. He looked lonesome and depressed as they pulled out of the parking lot. She knew that he was still terribly in love with her sister, Beth. They were planning to get married, but, unfortunately, while Roger was the agent for a rock band, he got mixed up with drugs and alcohol. Beth tried to get him to go into rehab, but he refused to admit that he had a problem. The last straw for her came when the tabloids started talking about his lurid affair with one of the singers in the group.

After their break-up, he resigned as the group's agent and wandered around for months, until one night, he landed in jail for public drunkenness. The judge sentenced him to a three-week's stay in a treatment center. It was the best thing that could have happened to him. Although Beth refused to get back together with him, she did encourage Jan to ask him to help her launch her career. Beth knew that Roger was still well known among the leading recording studios and could open some doors for Jan that otherwise might have taken years to get through.

Within two weeks of Jan's call to Roger, he had arranged for a recording session with a prominent record company. They signed her on immediately, and her career skyrocketed. Her first single was a song she had written herself. Amazingly, it was a major hit. After years of singing in bars and dance halls in Texas, it still shocked her that now she could fill a huge arena with fans who came from all over just to hear her. Even after two years of stardom, she was still trying to adjust to her new life, and she wasn't sure she liked it.

Chapter 2

It was barely daylight when Bill pulled the coach into the curved drive of the hotel and knocked on the door to Jan's bedroom in the motor home. "We're here, Jan. Do you want to go in, or do you just want to stay on the coach for a while longer?"

"Thanks, Bill," called Jan drowsily as she opened her door. "I think I'll go inside and get a couple more hours of sleep. Will you take care of getting the bags to my room?"

"I sure will. It looks like there's someone already standing outside the door of the coach anxiously awaiting the chance to help you. I'll go and tell him that you'll be out in a few minutes."

"Thanks. I just want to splash some water on my face and grab my overnight bag and my guitar. I'll be with you in a second."

Jan could hear Bill talking to the uniformed young man outside the coach. She grabbed what she needed for right now and climbed down to the pavement. The young man immediately reached for her bag and guitar.

"Thanks, but I'll carry the guitar," she smiled. "I'd appreciate it, though, if you would take my bag."

~~~~~

"No problem," said Richard flashing a broad smile. He couldn't believe his luck at being on duty when Jan Taylor arrived. He tried not to stare at her but couldn't help noticing how gorgeous she was, even without any makeup and dressed in an old flannel shirt and jeans. Her curly, dark auburn hair just barely touched her shoulders. In the early morning breeze, it blew softly across her face. Her skin was

13

flawless, and her green eyes glistened like emeralds. The breeze blew her shirt tight against her chest, outlining her shapely figure. Her slim jeans showed off her perfectly sculptured lower body, and he had to concentrate to keep his mind on the hotel room number he had been given. He led her through the lobby and stepped aside to let her enter the private elevator that led to the suites on the top floor.

"What's your name? Jan asked as the elevator door closed.

"I'm sorry. I forgot to introduce myself. I'm Richard Evans, at your service. If you need anything, don't hesitate to call the main desk. It's an honor to have you in the hotel," he babbled, realizing he sounded like a silly high school student instead of the third year vet student that he was. He had been working at the hotel part-time on the late-night shift for two years to earn money for school. One more year and he would be finished.

He knew Jan was not only a rising star in country music, but she was also an accomplished horsewoman. When he learned she would be staying at the hotel while she was in Oklahoma City, he scanned the huge catalog of the World Show entries and marked the classes she had entered. Last year her stallion had earned the coveted AQHA Versatility award in the Open Division. He had also been the Open Division Grand Champion in both reining and ranch trail for the past two years. Her ranch had entries for many of the other events but with different riders. He wondered how she balanced her personal and professional life. Building a bond with a horse and keeping it fit for competition takes a lot of time. She had been riding the same stallion for three years. *I find it hard to believe that she can build a relationship with such a powerful animal and yet bounce around from state-to-state on her tours,* he thought. *She probably owns a large horse farm and has dozens of trainers working for her. More than likely, she gets on the horse just long enough to compete. The animal is undoubtedly a push-button horse—so well trained that all she has to do is hold the reins and remember the pattern. Must be nice.*

~~~~~

He would discover later that he couldn't have been more wrong in his suppositions. True, Jan and her sisters did own a Texas ranch, but they worked it alone. They only had one foreman on the ranch and several part-time employees. Jan trained her own horses and didn't allow anyone but her niece Jamie even to groom her prize stud, Raven. The truth was that no one else wanted to groom him or even go near him. If anyone else tried to ride him, he quickly dislodged the would-be rider with no remorse. That's why it was so crucial for her to arrive a few days before she was to show him. Even though Jamie had been constantly working with him, he would need some attention from her before he was ready to enter the show ring.

"Here's your suite," said Richard, unlocking the door and handing her the key. "Would you like some ice or anything else?"

"No. I think I'm good." She smiled and offered him a tip.

"That's all right," he said gently shoving the tip back to her. "It's an honor just to get to spend a few minutes with you. I admire your horsemanship."

"My horsemanship?" Jan chuckled. "Well, now that's a switch—and one that I appreciate. It takes skill to be a good horsewoman; the singing career was just a gift from my dad."

"Oh, I like your vocals, too," he quickly replied. "I have your new album and several of your CD's, but

15

it's just that I'm a large animal vet student, so I pay close attention to the horse industry. You have some tough competition this year. I hope you can keep your title. I mean… I'm sure you'll be able to win again," he babbled, becoming more embarrassed by the moment.

Jan smiled at him, trying to ease his discomfort. "I've heard that there are several really good horses out to make sure that winning doesn't happen for me this year, but I intend to give it my best shot. I can't wait until I can get over to the World Show, so I can work my horse. I've been gone for a month, but my niece Jamie has been working him for me. You should stop by our stalls and meet her. She's still an undergrad but hopes to enter vet school next year."

"You really don't mind if I stop by? I'm interning with one of the veterinarians working the show, so I'll be there whenever I'm not in school or working here at nights. I'd love to see your stud up close. He's an amazing animal."

"Yes, he is, but he's also a handful, so make sure that one of us is with you before you try to get too close. I'll give you the cell number that I'll be using while I'm here. I get a new one every few weeks to preserve my privacy, but this number will be good for the time that I'm here. Give me a call when you're in the barns. I think we're in the Super Barn, and most of my classes are in the Jim Norick Arena, except for trail, which is in the Performance Arena. But, I'm not sure about that; I haven't seen the revised schedule of events," she said as she scrawled her number on the hotel pad. "I'll give you Jamie's number too, in case I get tied up with rehearsals. She can handle Raven as well as I can."

"Thank you so much, Miss Taylor. I promise to respect your privacy, but I would love to see the horse. Now I'll just get out of here, so you can get some rest. Thanks again," he repeated as he backed out the door.

Jan smiled at Richard's obvious excitement over her horse. She loved horses as much, if not more, than singing. Riding Raven across the top of the ridge that runs along the back fence line of their ranch was the most liberating experience ever. She loved riding him just as the sun was setting in the wide, Texas sky. They flew toward the sun as if they were chasing it, hoping to catch it before it disappeared over the horizon.

Raven seemed to enjoy their evening runs as much as she did. He would reach out as far as he could with his front legs and push with his powerful hind legs lengthening his stride to the limit. His nose pointed straight ahead, and his head and neck stretched in a straight line with the rest of his body as he raced with ease and pure joy. For Jan, it was like sitting on a low-flying rocket. Raven was a five-year-old great, great grandson of the famous thoroughbred, Three Bars. Although Three Bars was a thoroughbred, he was later bred to quarter horse mares and was eventually inducted into the American Quarter Horse Hall of Fame because of the long-line of successful AQHA champions he sired. Jan's older sister, Lacey, had just bred Raven with one of the mares on the ranch who had won some major quarter horse stakes races. They hoped that the in-foal mare would bring a high price at the World Show.

In her last email, Lacey indicated that the three sisters needed to do some serious talking about the future of the ranch. The downturn in the economy had caused a rapid dip in the sale of the performance and work horses that they bred. Their stock was growing, and profit from any sales they did make was small. She was hoping by extending their breeding program from only work and performance breeding to quarter horse race breeding that she could get higher prices for their foals and their stud fees to help with the dwindling cash flow for the ranch. Though Jan wanted to keep the mare and only sell the foal, Lacey had told her that they needed money now to help support their immediate needs at the ranch.

Lacey was the oldest of the three sisters; Jan was the youngest. For Jan, life had been relatively easy, but for Lacey, life had been unfair. Five years ago, their parents and Lacey's husband, Robert, had been killed in a tragic air crash. The three of them were on their way to the World Show, traveling in a private plane with several other horse people from Texas. They were going to the show ahead of the rigs that were hauling the horses to get the stalls and other provisions ready before the horses arrived. The plane went down after being struck by lightning, and everyone on board was killed.

Robert was the foundation on which everyone depended. He managed the ranch for her mom and dad and was a loving husband and father. The ranch was struggling a little before the accident, and after the crash, things didn't improve. Lacey assumed most of the responsibility for running the daily operations of the ranch and the breeding, and Jan focused on the training of their competition and work horses. Beth had little interest in the ranch but helped where she could. She was scared of most of the studs they had, even after living around them all her life. An accident as a child had caused her to shy away from anything to do with climbing on the back of a horse.

In the years immediately following the accident, Lacey was afraid they were going to lose their ranch. Several small, neighboring ranchers had already sold out to larger, more diversified ranches. Jan decided to pursue a professional career in music to help provide cash to make payments on their ranch. Now she was in debt herself and struggling to help with

18

the debts of the ranch.

"I need to get some sleep," she yawned, as she kicked off her boots and climbed into bed without changing her clothes.

Chapter 3

A light tap on her hotel door woke Jan from a sound sleep. "Who is it?" she muttered.

"Aunt Jan," whispered Jamie. "It's me."

Jan sat up and stumbled to the door. *How long have I been asleep*, she wondered. *It feels like seconds*. She flipped over the security hook and unlocked the door. Her niece Jamie lunged at her and nearly bowled her over with a giant hug. Jamie was the oldest of Lacey's two children. She was a beautiful brunette with sparkling brown eyes and a sweet disposition. As a college senior in biology through an online program at the University of Phoenix, she was awaiting acceptance in an online program to pursue a degree in Veterinary Medicine.

"I'm so glad to see you, Aunt Jan," Jamie whispered. "I thought this night would never end. Are you ready to head for the arena? I can't wait until you see Raven. He's rearing to go, and I do mean rearing. They're having a terrible time with him at the barn. I'm sure he'll calm right down as soon as he sees you. He has really missed you, almost as much as I have," she babbled as Jan still tried to get her eyes focused and process everything her niece was chattering about.

"What time is it?" Jan asked as she returned her niece's embrace.

"It's ten after five. What time did you get here?" asked Jamie.

"Four-thirty, I think, or shortly after." She yawned, realizing that it had actually only been minutes since she lay down. "Are you sure you want to head for the

20

arena so soon? It's not even daylight yet?"

"Sure, I'm ready. When you're at the ranch, we're always in the barn by now. You look like you're all ready to go, except for your wig and sun glasses. Where are your bags?"

"I don't think they've had time to unload them yet. I'll call down to the main desk, and I'm sure that young bell-boy will be only too happy to bring them up. Wait 'till you see him. It should brighten up your outlook on life—handsome, third year, large animal vet student."

"I don't have time for boys, Aunt Jan. I'm too much like you. Horses are my only love."

"Hmm," groaned Jan. "I'm not sure you have me pegged as clearly as you think you do. I love horses, but I am not totally anti-men. I just haven't met Mr. Right yet. I hope that he'll come along soon before I lose my...never mind. I'll just call the desk."

Richard answered the phone on the first ring. "Bell Captain's Desk, Richard Evans speaking," he announced. "Of course, I'll bring them up right away. I just thought you would be still sleeping," he said, immediately regretting his familiarity with the famous star.

Within moments, another knock on Jan's suite announced the arrival of Richard with her bags.

"That was quick," said Jan, smiling at Richard's eagerness to please. "Richard, this is my niece Jamie Livingston. I told her that you might be calling her to connect with Raven." Then, turning to Jamie, who was busy fussing with her iPad, she continued, "Jamie, this is Richard Evans the young vet student I was telling you about."

"Hi," replied Jamie, without looking up.

21

"Hello," muttered Richard totally awestruck by Jamie's beauty. She was tall and thin like her Aunt with the same alluring figure, but her long, dark hair was straight and as shiny as highly polished, black onyx.

"Jamie, for heaven's sake, put that crazy iPad down and join us in real time here," teased Jan. "I'm sorry for her rudeness, Richard. She's been around horses most of her life and is obviously a little rusty when it comes to communicating with humans."

"I'm sorry," apologized Jamie. "I was trying to download your new album, so I'm not sure why you'd mind me fussing with my iPad." As she looked up, her attitude suddenly shifted. She quickly scanned Richard's tall, well-defined body and his handsome face. His eyes and hair were dark like hers, and he gazed at her with a kind, friendly expression. "It's nice to meet you, Richard. I'll look forward to showing Raven off to you," she said jumping up and flashing him her most charming smile.

Jan chuckled to herself as she watched the transparent attraction between the two young people. *Oh, to be that young again and so quick to fall madly in love*, she thought. "Just put the luggage over there, Richard," she suggested and once again offered him a tip that he refused.

"OK. I guess I'd better let you ladies get over to the arena. I hope to give you a call when I get out of class," he said directing his gaze at Jamie. Jan guessed that he would not be calling her number any time soon.

After he left the room, Jamie squealed with sheer delight. "Now he is someone I could give up horses for. But, isn't it great—he loves horses, too. I could have the best of both worlds with him. I think I'm in love!" she screeched.

"Whoa, sweetheart," cautioned Jan. "Let's not leap before we look more carefully. We don't know anything about him, and there'll be lots of young cowboys following you around during this next couple of weeks. I have to admit, though, he looks like a good catch. If I were about five years younger, I think I would give you a run for your money."

"Thank goodness, you aren't. I could never compete against you. You're still a knockout, even in your mid-thirties."

"Early-thirties," corrected Jan. "Come on, let's get out of here." She opened a small box and took out a short, blonde wig that she plopped on her head, tucking her red curls up underneath. "Do you like my new wig? I thought I would see if blondes really do have more fun."

"Well, for someone who wants to be incognito, you certainly chose a mighty pretty wig. You should have gone for a mousey brown," teased Jamie.

"Shush, let's get out of here." Jan plopped her Stetson on top of the wig. "I hope the wig doesn't fly off with the hat. That should really impress the judges and unsuspecting by-standers."

"You're not going to wear a wig while you're showing, are you? You're already listed in the program, so everyone will be coming to see your classes just as they have done for the past two years. You won't be able to hide behind some blonde wig once they know you're in the show ring."

"I'm not sure. It depends on how lucky I get as a blonde." Jan laughed and led the way out of the suite into the hall. "By the way, does your mom know you're going to the arena at this hour? And, what about Justin? Won't he be hurt when he finds out we left without him?"

"I left mom a note, and Justin spent the night over at Fair Park in the trailer. He was sure you would come there first, so he wanted to be there to greet you. I knew you would want to come here first, so I didn't bother to correct him. Now, I get to watch him burn when he discovers that I saw you first."

"You're evil," teased Jan, hugging her ornery niece. "And, how are we getting to the arena? I don't want to show up out there in my motor coach, although Bill will eventually be taking it over and parking it on the grounds, so we can use it while we're there."

"We rented a pick-up. The dualies and cabs are too tall for the hotel garage. I drove back from the arena with Mom and Beth. We'll have to come back and get them when they finally get up."

"Sounds great, but I want to drive. I haven't been behind the wheel of a pick-up for a month, and I miss it," said Jan.

"Are you sure you can still drive a stick-shift? We didn't rent an automatic."

"Like riding a bike—once you learn you never forget how."

Chapter 4

As they entered the barn, Jan could already hear Raven's distinctive whinny—actually it sounded more like a scream.

"You sure were right. He's out of sorts." Jan took off running down the aisle toward Raven's stall. "That's his *'help me'* scream," she called over her shoulder.

"You can actually distinguish between his whinnies?" said Jamie running beside her aunt. "You're joking, right?"

"Sure, I can tell the difference between his whinnies, and I'm disappointed that you can't. You'd better start listening to your horses if you intend to become a vet." Jan started a low, whistling sound, as they got closer to Raven's stall. Amazingly, the frantic whinny stopped, and a soft nicker and a rattling of the stall door replaced it.

When they got to his stall, Raven was frantically pacing in the small area. When he heard Jan's voice, he reared and pawed the air in total joy.

"Easy there, fellow," whispered Jan. "I've missed you, too." She slowly slid back the U-bolt on the stall door and waited until Raven settled himself before she reached out to let him sniff her hand as she rubbed his velvety muzzle. "Don't even think about nipping at me," she admonished, as Raven began to nibble on her hand. "Have they been mistreating you while I was gone?" she whispered, slowly moving her hand over his withers and down his strong, sleek back. Her disciplined hands could tell that he was still tense and would require a good work out in the circle pen before he would be ready for her to ride him.

25

Jamie stood in admiration, watching as her aunt easily calmed the previously out-of-control animal. Although Raven would allow Jamie to ride him, she was never able to calm him the way her aunt could. She knew that he trusted her, but not the way he trusted Jan. He was truly a one-woman horse—nice for Jan, but it made it extremely difficult for his other handlers.

"Hey, you two, why didn't y'all come by the trailer to get me?" demanded Justin, jogging down the aisle toward the two women. "I knew you were in here when I heard Raven stop his insidious screams. I could hear him all night clear outside. He kept me and everyone else in the camp grounds awake."

"Hey, Buddy," called out Jan from inside the stall. "Sorry about not stopping by to get you, but I could hear Raven's cries for help as soon as I stepped out of the pick-up. Hang on a minute, so I can get my hug from you. I just about have him calmed down enough to lead him out of the stall."

"Where did you get that ridiculous blonde wig?" asked Justin. "Surely, you don't intend to wear that around here, do you? Everyone already knows you're going to be here, so there's no use in trying to disguise yourself."

"What? You don't like this expensive wig. It cost me some big bucks." Jan laughed. "Actually, you're probably right; it's uncomfortable under my hat anyway. Reaching up she pulled off her hat and rested it on Raven's head while she pulled off the wig and handed it through the stall door to Jamie. "Put it in one of the hat boxes in the tack room, but be careful with it. I wasn't kidding about it being expensive."

"I can't believe that crazy horse lets you put a hat on his head," complained Justin. "He won't let anyone else even begin to touch his ears. He's really the worse behaved horse we have in any of the barns. You've spoiled him."

"I have not spoiled him. I know better than to spoil any horse. He just has a keen sense about who likes him, and who doesn't. Obviously, he knows that you don't care for him."

"Whatever. The next time you go on tour, I'm going to attach a horse trailer to the back of that motor coach, so you can take him with you," he teased.

"I'm sure he won't like traipsing across hundreds of miles any more than I do. And, he would hate living in a different barn every other night."

"Poor you," teased Justin. "I'd give anything to do what you do, see what you see, and live like you live."

"Oh, yeah? Well, next summer I just might drag you along with me for a couple of weeks. I bet you that, within a week, you would be bored out of your skull and beg to get back to some wide-open spaces. Now hand me his halter and lead rope. I think I have him rubbed down enough to take him over to the circle pen and turn him loose."

Jan carefully slipped the halter over Raven's head and attached the lead rope on the side of the halter.

"Aren't you going to put the chain over his nose?" asked Justin. "You'll never be able to control him with it hooked on the side."

"Oh no? Just watch me." Jan smiled at Justin's doubtful look, and then she led Raven out of the stall and down the aisle. Raven followed along next to her, keeping in perfect stride with the pace that she set for him. Justin marveled at the mannerly horse that

27

crossed the driveway toward the group of circle pens set up as exercise rings. Raven never once reared or pulled back on the lead rope. He stayed right beside Jan and presented a perfect disciplined appearance.

"What has she got that I don't have?" moaned Justin. "True, I don't like that horse, but, surely, he doesn't really know that I don't like him."

"Oh yes, he does," argued Jamie. "You cop an attitude every time you get near him. It's almost like you think he's a challenge to your manhood, little brother," she teased.

"Oh, shut up, Jamie. You don't know what you're talking about," pouted Justin. "And quit calling me, your *little* brother. You may be two years older than I am, but I'm a good six inches taller than you."

"Sorry. I stand corrected. You no longer are my *little* brother, but, of course, you'll always be my *younger* brother." She laughed and poked him in the side with her elbow.

Once inside of the circle pen, Jan turned Raven loose. No one else was around, so she didn't feel the need to tether him on a lunge line. Raven took off as if he were shot from a cannon. He bucked, reared, and jumped around for pure joy. The three of them watched him as he played, admiring his shiny black coat; his well-toned, muscled body; and his enormous size. At just over 17 hands, he was certainly an impressive example of magnificent beauty. Every buyer who came to the ranch wanted to purchase him—that is, until the prospective buyers got too near his stall. Then, he would show off his poor temperament, and they would quickly shy away. It was almost as if he purposefully misbehaved, so he wouldn't be sold. Of course, everyone associated with the ranch knew that Jan would never sell him. He was born on the ranch the same year that her parents and their father had died, and he would probably be buried on it.

After giving him a little playtime, Jan whistled to him, and he quickly trotted over to the gate where she stood waiting for him. She reached up, grabbed his halter, and led him to the center of the pen. Then, she made a soft, clicking sound with her tongue against the roof of her mouth, and he immediately went to the rail and began a slow trot around the perimeter of the pen with Jan turning to watch his stride. After several minutes, she clicked again, and he quickly changed his gait to a slow canter.

"Whoa," called Jan softly. Raven skidded to an immediate stop and turned to trot toward her in the middle of the pen. She turned him around and clicked, and he trotted off, circling the pen in the opposite direction. After about twenty minutes of exercising him, she called him to the center of the pen again. Fastening the lead-line on his halter, she led him around the pen at a slow walk for several minutes until he had cooled down. Finally, she led him back to the stall with Jamie and Justin following behind her. They remained in complete awe of her ability to handle such a powerful horse.

"Get me his grooming tools, will you, Jamie?" Jan asked as she connected Raven's halter to the tie ropes on each side of the aisle. She patted him gently on the neck while she rubbed his forehead. "I want to brush him down again before I saddle him. Are you two going to saddle your mounts, so we can work out together?"

"If I tried to work my horse at this hour in the morning, he would think I'd gone nuts," replied Justin. "I'm not showing today, so I thought I would work him at noon. Most of the pretty cowgirls start showing up in the practice arenas around eleven o'clock. I try to time my workouts, so I can pick out my lunch partner," he bragged.

"You're disgusting," muttered Jamie as she handed Raven's grooming box to Jan.

Every horse had personal grooming tools and saddle blankets. Saddles were personalized by rider, not by horse, but everything else including halters, lunge lines, and lead ropes was separated by horse. The ranch rented additional stalls for tack rooms, dressing rooms, and eating and entertainment areas. They reserved two aisles for their exclusive use during the entire show. This year, they brought four of their performance horses, four halter horses, and three yearlings to sell along with the in-foul mare. Every year, it cost them a bundle to come to the World Show, but it was the best advertisement for the ranch and their breeding program that they could buy. The exposure they got at the show was well worth the cost of bringing the horses.

"I'll just watch you work Raven today," said Jamie. "Tomorrow, I'll exercise Brandy when you exercise Raven. The two of them get along pretty well, as long as Brandy doesn't crowd Raven."

"I need to get Raven used to working with the mares and other stallions, so he will behave in the show ring. We might want to give him a second workout later today when Justin works out—that is, if you don't think we'll cramp your style by being in the same workout arena as you, Justin," Jan teased.

"Well, to be completely honest, I'd rather you not use the same workout arena as me. If girls see you talking to me, they may not go out with me just because of me, if you know what I mean."

"Oh, so my fame as a country singer is actually a handicap to you, is it?"

"Well, let's just say, that I only use our

relationship as a ploy when I can't get the attention I want just by being me, which really isn't very often," he bragged.

"Oh, give us a break," gagged Jamie. "You are without a doubt the most arrogant of the male species I have ever met; and believe me, I've met quite a few arrogant males."

"And, what about you, Jamie? Does my fame interfere with your personal relationships?"

"Heck no; I can tell in a heartbeat if someone is sideling up to me to get a better look at you, and I drop them like a hot potato," proclaimed Jamie proudly.

"And pray, Miss Enlightened One, how can you tell that they are more interested in our famous aunt than you?" mocked Justin.

"Well first, they seem to be looking around a lot and not making any real eye contact with me. Then, they're usually stupid enough to ask me early in the conversation if it is true that my aunt is Jan Taylor. On the other hand, take that Richard Evans this morning, the bell-hop at the hotel—he completely ignored you, Aunt Jan, once he got a look at me. No offense."

"None taken," replied Jan laughing. "You're absolutely right. Once he got a look at you, he never even glanced my way. I gave him both of our cell numbers, but he looked straight at you when he said he would call later."

"C'mon on, give me a break," groaned Justin. "This guy must be nuts. Jamie can't even begin to hold a candle to you in looks or personality. The guy must be blind or completely stupid," he taunted.

"Thanks a lot, brother dear," pouted Jamie tossing a soft brush at Justin and causing Raven to jump.

31

"Hey, no horse-play in the barn," reminded Jan as she softly stroked Raven on the neck. "Justin, why don't you use your manly prowess to fetch me my work saddle and Raven's working bridle?"

"And don't mess up the organization in the tack room, Justin," called Jamie. "You left everything in a mess last night, and I had to spend a half an hour putting things back where they belonged. When we start showing, we won't have much time between classes and horses, so, please, you two, put things back where they belong."

"Yes, Mam," answered Jan and Justin in unison.

"All kidding aside, Jamie, I appreciate you keeping us all organized," said Jan tossing Jamie a kiss to soothe her wounded pride. "It will be a disaster if we can't find things easily once our classes start."

Jan quickly saddled and bridled Raven, and the threesome walked out into the fresh morning air with Jan leading Raven. It was a little warmer than the typical November morning in Oklahoma, but it felt chilly after the heat of the barn.

Jan easily swung herself up into the saddle and leaned over to steady the stirrups while she slipped her foot into one and then the other. Raven stood perfectly still, waiting for a cue from her before he moved. "Jamie, watch his right front leg. I thought he was favoring it a little this morning. I wouldn't be surprised if he didn't bruise it rearing in the stall. He might have hit it on the metal edge."

"That's all we would need. If he gets disqualified here, there goes another All Around for him and for the barn," groaned Jamie. "That certainly won't help our financial woes."

Jan frowned, surprised that Jamie was aware

of the financial problems with the ranch. *Things must be more desperate than Lacey let on through her emails and phone calls.*

Chapter 5

After Raven's workout, Jan headed back to the hotel with Jamie. Justin decided to stay behind and muck out the stalls. On the way back, Lacey called Jamie on her cell phone and told them to join her for breakfast. When she met them in the hotel lobby, Jan was shocked at her appearance. In just the short time that she had been on tour, Lacey had clearly lost weight and looked considerably older than her forty years.

"Hey, Sis," smiled Lacey giving Jan a warm hug. "How's my famous, little sister? You look great, but you smell like Raven." she teased. "I take it you've already had a workout with that monster."

"Yes, thanks to Jamie we got an early start." Jan smiled at her sister but continued to worry about Lacey's loss of weight and her haggard appearance. "What about you? Have you been losing weight on purpose?"

"No, she hasn't," interrupted Jamie. "She just never eats and spends most of the night pacing back and forth in her room. I told her that she looks like she's aged twenty years in the past month. It's the darn ranch. It's going to kill her."

"Jamie, please. Come on, we're here to have fun and to enjoy Jan while she's here. Let's not ruin it by talking about ranch worries before breakfast. Anyway, how do you know that I pace back-and-forth at night?"

"My room is right next to yours, for gosh sakes. I hear you pacing around all the time. I'm surprised that I don't have bags under my eyes down to my knees, too."

34

"Let's just go and get some breakfast," said Lacey. "Where's Justin? Didn't you wake him up while you were out there? He'll be furious."

"He met us in the barn," said Jamie. "He said he wanted to stay and clean the stalls. He probably wants to get his aisle done so he can be free to chase his little cowgirls all afternoon."

"His aisle?" asked Jan. "What's that about?"

"We each agreed to take an aisle to keep clean," said Jamie. "Works out better that way—we don't end up arguing about who has to do which stall."

"OK," said Jan. "Let's go get some food, and then, Lacey, you and I will go wake up our *Sleeping-Beauty* sister and have a long talk. Just the three of us," she emphasized giving her niece a sympathetic grin.

"Why just the three of you?" pouted Jamie. "The ranch is just as much a part of my future as it is yours."

"Well, when you start contributing to the revenue of the ranch, then you can attend our business meetings, young lady," said Lacey, obviously irritated by her daughter's demanding tone. "You had better enjoy your current, carefree life—it will soon be over once you graduate and hit the real world."

"Sorry," apologized Jamie. "I didn't mean to sound pushy."

The remainder of the breakfast was spent going over the schedule of events and working out who was to be *where* to help with *what*. Their show schedule was hectic starting the day after tomorrow and continuing through Friday night when Jan had to leave again. Luckily, her events fell in the same week, so she could try to get as many points for Raven as possible during the time she was here. She would

35

have to win almost every one of her events if she was to earn enough points on him for the All Around. Hopefully, his right foreleg would be okay after some rest today. Jamie had agreed that he was favoring it a little, and Jan had decided that it was rather warm when she rubbed him down after the workout. They had both agreed to give the vet a call as soon as they finished eating.

After breakfast, Lacey and Jan headed to Beth's room to wake her and to have the conversation about the future of the ranch that was weighing heavily on both Jan and Lacey's minds.

"I tried to talk Roger in to coming to the show," Jan remarked as they exited the elevator and headed to Beth's room. "He's still in love with her but thinks Beth will never give him another chance."

"I don't know about that," commented Lacey. "Wait 'til you see Beth's latest paintings."

"What do you mean?" asked Jan. "What do her paintings have to do with Roger?"

"You'll see," replied Lacey.

Beth was a talented artist and had a highly successful career as a Western painter. Many collectors and dealers sought her paintings. She did a lot of business at the World Show, typically selling her work and getting enough commissioned works to support her for the year. Each year, she had a booth at the show and spent the whole time talking with patrons while she worked on a painting that represented the theme of the show. She always donated the painting to a charity for abused animals, and they auctioned it off.

At the ranch, she had built a beautiful studio with living quarters. When she wasn't visiting another ranch to complete a commissioned work, she spent her entire life inside her studio, rarely visiting the barns or helping out on the ranch. She did contribute some of her earnings to running the ranch, but years ago, she had made it perfectly clear to her parents and sisters that she was not—nor never would be—a horsewoman. She painted them beautifully but rarely touched the horses.

Jan knew that the reason for Beth's distrust of horses stemmed from a tragic fall during a jumping competition when she was younger. For months following her accident, she had been confined to a wheel chair, and it was only through intensive therapy and expensive medical treatment that she eventually was able to walk again. Their parents spent almost everything they earned on surgeries and therapy for her. Their mother encouraged Beth to take up painting while she was going through all of the painful treatments. Her painting kept her from giving up on life, and she buried herself in it to fight off the depression and pain. Although she walks with a cane, she is now able to get around without assistance; however, she is still somewhat of a recluse.

Beth met Roger Allen when she was commissioned to paint the ranch house of one of the members of a band that he was representing. Roger was also staying at that ranch, relaxing between gigs. Beth remained at the ranch for several weeks, sketching and taking pictures of the house and the surrounding landscape. She always liked to get to know her patron so that the final painting reflected his or her presence. She had an uncanny way of portraying the karma of the client in her artwork.

As Jan and Roger were riding together in the tour bus a month or so ago, he had confessed to Jan that, the very first time he saw Beth, he was immediately struck by her natural beauty and by her quiet, somewhat shy personality. He talked about Beth's hair, describing it as being as dark as the

37

desert night, and he described her eyes as the lightest shade of blue he had ever seen. *'Her skin is pale and soft, like a fresh lilly'* he had said. He confessed that he had spent the whole time he was at the ranch just watching her work, silently enjoying the ambiance that surrounded her. Before he left, he had told her that he was madly in love with her and had asked her to marry him. To everyone's surprise, Beth had accepted his offer without hesitation.

Jan remembered how she and Lacey had questioned her about such a hasty decision to marry someone she hardly knew. Beth had argued that he was an exciting man. He was everything she wasn't—fun-loving, widely traveled, and athletic. He was respected in the music industry, and he was handsome with a sincere desire to protect her. *'Why shouldn't I want to marry someone like him?'* she had asked.

At first, their engagement went smoothly. Roger visited Beth at their ranch every time he could, and Beth began to come out of her self-imposed isolation. She even accompanied him on the road on two occasions, getting some personal exposure from the media, which increased her notoriety among art dealers and collectors. As time went on, Beth noticed that Roger was drinking more heavily than usual, and she had, on several occasions, caught him smoking marijuana with other band members. He was working excessively long hours trying to resolve the bickering between the members of the band.

Eventually, the tabloids began reporting on the potential break-up of the band and exploited Roger and one of the back-up singers in some torrid love triangle with the lead guitarist. Though Roger and others involved in the expose' tried to convince Beth that it was all a lie, she had enough of his drinking and long absences and could no longer see her future as part of Roger's lifestyle. She broke off the engagement two years ago. Following the break-up, Jan could only watch as she sank deeper into her reclusiveness and avoided association with any other male, though many tried to spark her interest.

Lacey knocked on the door to Beth's room. "Come-on, Sleepy-head, we know you're in there. I have a nice surprise for you."

They could hear the thumping of Beth's cane as she hurried to open the door.

"Hey, Sis," said Jan, hugging Beth. "You're looking svelte as usual."

"Jan, I'm so glad to see you," responded Beth, hugging her tightly. "I've missed you more this time than ever. How's the tour going? *Billboard Magazine* is sure praising your successes. They say you're a shoo-in for the Best Young Artist of the Year Award."

"Beth, you should know by now that you can't believe everything you read in print," joked Jan. She was immediately sorry that she had said what she did when she noticed the pain in Beth's eyes. "Anyway, the tour is grueling, and I can't wait to get back home. Just three more stops to go, so I'll be home for the Christmas holidays."

"Are you hungry, Beth?" asked Lacey. "Why don't you call for room service, so we can have this dreaded conversation about the ranch? I know we'll all enjoy the show much better, if we get this over with."

"Can't we just take a few minutes to catch up with Jan before we start being so serious? You need to relax a little, Lacey. Loosen up, and start to enjoy life a little again," chided Beth.

"Well, someone has to worry about paying the bills," stormed Lacey, clearly hurt by Beth's refusal to pay attention to what was happening around her. "We can't all go traipsing across the country or shut ourselves up in our own little retreat."

"Whoa, whoa," said Jan. "What's going on here, Lacey? Tell me, are things that bad?"

Lacey burst into tears and threw herself across the bed. She continued to cry uncontrollably for several minutes, refusing to respond to either of her sisters' reassurances and apologies. Finally, she began to regain some composure. "I'm selling off the 200 acres on the west end of the ranch. It's the only way we can get enough cash to get caught up with the mortgage and the taxes," she blurted out.

"What? You're selling off some of the ranch? You just can't do that." Jan was shocked that such a decision had been made without her input. "How much do you need? I've been making the monthly mortgage payments. I don't understand."

"It's not enough, Jan. I appreciate the fact that you're already making our monthly payments, but the bank is calling in the balloon payment that was part of the loan agreement when Dad re-financed after Beth's accident. We'll need all of our savings and the money from the sale of the land just to keep the bank from foreclosing on us."

"So, this is all my fault," bellowed Beth.

"Oh, for Pete's sake, Beth," shouted Lacey. "None of this is your fault. I don't think you can possibly take the blame for the failures of the banking industry and the sagging financial situation of the country. We aren't the only ones in this mess. A lot of the smaller ranches around us have sold land to Brett Kendall. He's the only rancher who is surviving this chaos. He has offered to buy our land since it borders the Connor's ranch that he recently purchased and is now living on."

"How magnanimous of him—who is he anyway? I've never heard of him before," fumed Jan.

Lacey sighed and got up from the bed. "He's a wealthy oil man who owns a lot of property along the coast. He wanted to diversify his holdings, so he has ventured into the horse industry. He started out breeding thoroughbreds and has a huge horse farm in Kentucky. I guess he wants to try his hand at quarter horse racing too. Unfortunately, he picked the wrong time to expand his horse business."

"What could he possibly want with that piece of land?" stormed Jan. "It's not flat enough for racing, and it's too dry for good pasture most of the year. I don't like him, and I don't even know him."

"You haven't seen him yet," chided Beth. "He's quite a looker. I'd like to have a chance to paint him. He has a chiseled jaw, dark hair with just a touch of gray at the temples, and pale, blue eyes that could penetrate a steel door."

"The land he wants has a nice creek running through it, and it borders his own property," responded Lacey sighing and shaking her head at Beth's typical nonchalant attitude. "He's actually trying to help us and the other ranchers out. He has purchased a lot of acreage, trying to help the other small ranchers survive. He signs an agreement that he will re-sell the property back to the owners upon their request at the original sale price. Jim likes him a lot. In fact, Jim is working for Mr. Kendall to help me cut down on the payroll at home. He still helps out by coming over every night and working in the barns. I just couldn't keep him on full-time right now.

Jim Cordrey was the foreman of their ranch and had been working for them for years. He and Lacey's husband grew up together in Texas and stayed friends until Robert's death. At one point in her life, Lacey wasn't sure which of the two she wanted to marry, but, in the end, Robert proposed first, and Jim graciously stepped aside.

"You mean you've been running the ranch alone for the past month?" moaned Jan. "Why didn't you tell me?"

"What could you have possibly done? You have a right to your career, and you certainly couldn't have canceled your tour to come home and clean out stalls. Jamie and Justin have been great, and Jim is unbelievably supportive. I know I couldn't make it without him. He's been my rock since Robert died."

"Maybe you two should get married, then our payroll problems would be solved," teased Beth.

"For gods sake, Beth. Can't you be serious for even a minute?" Lacey glared at her.

"I *am* serious. You would have to be blind not to notice that he loves you. The poor guy has waited long enough for you to get around to him. He's killing himself working two jobs just to stay close to you. Give him a break. Marry him!" Beth screeched.

"Let's stay focused here," reminded Jan. "Lacey, do you have the actual facts and figures of what we owe? I would prefer not to sell the land if we don't have to."

"It's too late, Jan. I already signed the papers. Remember that you two gave me full power-of-attorney for the ranch, and I exercised it. Jim and I discussed this for weeks and decided this was the easiest fix to our current situation. Brett promised he would sell the property back to us at any time we want it."

"Well, then, I guess there's nothing else to talk about. I'm out of here," stormed Jan.

42

"Jan, please don't be mad at me," pleaded Lacey. "I know it's the right thing for all of us right now. You've been more than generous with your money, but we can't go on living off you. We need to help, too. I know you have your own financial worries now. Let me worry about the ranch. I promise I won't sell any more of the land without talking it over with you first."

"I'm not mad at you, Lacey. I trust you, and I trust Jim. I know you will do what is right; it's Brett Kendall, I don't trust. Somewhere along the way, I've learned that *if something is too good to be true, then it probably is.*"

"Would you like to meet him?" asked Lacey. "I know he's here. He even brought Jim with him and told him to spend as much time as he needed to help us out. Jim drove one of our rigs, and Mr. Kendall had one of his other men drive our other rig, so I just had to drive the diesel with the fifth wheel. He really has been a wonderful neighbor, and I do trust him. Why don't I see if Jim can arrange for a dinner between the two of you? You need to find out for yourself what kind of man he is."

"I don't think so," snarled Jan. "I don't think I'll have much time for late-night dinners between my show and workout schedules. And, don't forget I agreed to do a performance in the arena before I leave. Now, unless you ladies have any more bad news to share with me, I'm going to try to get some rest for a couple of hours before heading out to the barn. I think I have my own worries with Raven. Beth, I'll stop by at your booth. I want to see your latest paintings. Are you in the same place as always?"

"Yep, the same spot for the past ten years," answered Beth tossing Jan a sympathetic smile. She knew how much Jan loved the ranch and understood her disappointment at hearing that Lacey had sold a portion of it to a stranger.

"Lacey, you need to go and get some rest." Jan reached out and took hold of her older sister's hand. "I'm sorry you thought you had to go through all this alone. Please don't ever think that I can't be bothered or that I don't care. I do care, probably more than anyone. The ranch isn't just a business to me or just a place to live. It's *me*. It's who I am. I sing for the ranch, and I don't like being away from it—that's one thing I have discovered on this tour. But, I can't help if I don't know what's going on. It's just that I didn't know how bleak things were. Please keep me in the loop from now on. I'll kick in whatever it takes to keep the ranch. I want to do that." She smiled and gave Lacey a quick hug as she left.

Why is life so complicated, she wondered as she headed back to her room. *Money, money, money. It's always about money.*

Chapter 6

Back in her room, Jan flopped across the bed wanting desperately to fall asleep and escape from thinking. She grabbed a pillow and flipped it over, punching it in the middle with her fist. She flipped it again and then threw it across the room. Grabbing a second one, she slapped it over the back of her head and buried her face in the soft sheets. "Sleep, sleep, sleep," she whispered. After several minutes of fighting with the pillow and twisting and turning on the bed, she rolled over and curled up in a fetal position, tightly hugging the pillow to her chest. Exhaustion finally replaced her anger, disappointment, and worry, and she drifted off to sleep only to find herself in the middle of a chaotic dream.

Disjointed images flashed through her mind—images of the ranch with a For Sale sign at the gate and a tall man, wearing a gigantic black Stetson, standing there with dollar bills hanging out of his pockets. He was handing a suitcase full of money to Lacey, who was all bent over and leaning on a crooked cane. Straggly gray hair partially covered her aged face. She saw herself beating on a man with her guitar. The man seemed to be trying to push Raven into a trailer while Beth was sitting along the side of the driveway calmly painting a picture of the chaos. Raven suddenly reared and made a wild, high pitched scream that echoed across the hills as the sun disappeared from the sky.

The piercing sound of Raven's cry immediately caused Jan to sit straight up and leap out of bed. Her shirt was wet with perspiration and her head was pounding. For a minute, she just stood there totally disoriented by her surroundings. Finally, she plopped back down on the bed. "Thank goodness. What a horrible dream. I've got to get dressed and get out of here," she decided. She reached for the phone and dialed the concierge desk.

"Richard Evans speaking, how can I help you, Miss Taylor."

"Richard, thank goodness you're still there. Can you make arrangements for a rental pick-up truck to be delivered to the hotel?"

"Sure. I'll get one here right away. Do you have preferences for type, color, or make?"

"Just make it a straight-shift with cabin room for at least four. I don't care about color or anything else. Let me know when it gets here, and I'll come down to sign the papers. Thanks."

"No problem. I'll wait until it gets here before I take off for class."

"No, you don't need to wait around. I don't want to keep you or make you late."

"It's not a problem. I'll wait."

Jan hung up the phone and headed for the shower. "He's such a nice kid," she muttered. "Why can't everyone be that accommodating?" She sighed as she dropped her baggy shirt on to the floor and stepped into the warm, gentle water spray, letting it wash away the tension and disappointment of her conversation with Lacey and the horror of her nightmare.

As she stepped out of the shower, the phone rang. She grabbed it on the first ring, expecting it to be Richard calling about the truck.

"Aunt Jan," said Justin sounding out of breath. "You need to get back to the barn right away."

"Justin, what's going on? You sound like you've been running a race. What is it?"

"It's Raven—he's gone," shouted Justin into the phone.

"Gone? What do you mean he's gone?" asked Jan.

"Just get over here. His stall is empty, and Jim and I have been looking everywhere for him, but he's just not anywhere on the grounds."

"My god, Justin. I'll be right there."

"I've called Mom and Jamie; they're waiting for you in the truck, in front of the hotel. Hurry, please," he begged.

Jan slammed the phone down and grabbed a shirt and a pair of clean jeans from the suitcase. Her hair was still soaking wet, and she didn't' take time even to run a comb through it. She slapped her sunglasses on and grabbed her hat and boots and headed barefoot out the door. Richard stepped out of the elevator just as she headed toward it.

"Jamie told me," he said.

"Thanks for bringing the elevator up. I can't believe this. How could a huge, black stallion just disappear?" she said as the elevator door closed behind her.

"Is there anything I can do?" asked Richard feeling useless.

"Just get this damn elevator down to the lobby," she shouted. She leaned back against the wall trying to shove her foot into a boot and keep from falling over as the elevator jerked and started its slow decent.

When they reached the lobby, she bolted out of

the elevator toward the glass door of the hotel entrance swinging one boot in the air and running across the floor with one bare foot. She jumped into the truck next to Jamie, and the truck squealed out of the driveway.

"How could this happen?" she demanded, staring at Lacey. "Where was Jim? Didn't you hire any security for the barn?"

"Don't yell at mom," shouted Jamie. "It isn't her fault. We couldn't afford the expense of a full-time security guard. It's as simple as that. We've never had any problems here before. You know that."

"Sorry, sorry," muttered Jan. "I don't know what I'm doing. I'm just hysterical. Raven is everything to me; I can't help it."

"It's okay, Jan. We'll find him," said Lacey calmly. "I know how important he is to you. He's important to all of us. Don't forget the he's our main income source for our breeding program. We're all worried."

"He's not just an income source to me," said Jan disgustedly.

"Look you two," shouted Jamie. "Why don't both of you just shush."

"You're right, Jamie. Sorry, Lacey. I didn't mean to accuse you."

"Shush!" yelled Jamie again as they roared into the parking lot of the show grounds. Lacey turned the truck so quickly that Jan thought she was going to fall out the door. "Geez, Mom, don't flip this thing over," screeched Jamie clinging to Jan.

Justin came running toward them when they pulled up to the barn door. He was pale and soaking wet with perspiration. Behind him, Jan could see Jim and another tall, slender man standing in the doorway

48

of the barn. Next to them were standing two uniformed officers.

"Aunt Jan, I think we know what happened," blurted out Justin. "Mr. Kendall thinks he knows who took Raven."

"Mr. Kendall? What does he have to do with this?" shouted Jan, staring at the man standing next to Jim Cordrey.

"Raven was bred to one of his prize mares," answered Lacey. "We gave him a free stud service since he lets Jim come over and help us out. I didn't tell you that before because I knew it would make you mad. He tried to pay me, but I wouldn't take the money."

Jan whirled around to face Lacey. "Is there anything else you would like to tell me about Mr. Kendall? Is he sleeping with you too?"

Lacey reached out and slapped Jan hard across the face. "Don't you ever say anything like that to me again. I'll forgive you this time because I know you're half nuts worrying about Raven, but don't you ever accuse me of sleeping with another man—ever," she screeched with tears streaming down her cheeks.

Jamie grabbed her mother's arm and pulled her toward the barn. She turned around to glare at Jan, who just sank to the ground, rubbing her stinging cheek and sobbing out of control. Justin sat down on the ground next to her and put his arm around her. "It's okay, Aunt Jan. I know you didn't mean it. We'll find Raven. I know we will."

Jan leaned against his shoulder and continued to sob like a baby. He wrapped both arms around her and rocked her back and forth until she stopped crying.

"I, I'm sorry, Justin. I didn't mean to be so hateful

to your mom. I was way out of line. I really have no excuse. It's just that my life is all mixed up right now. I don't know what the heck I'm doing running around the country singing to people I can't even see because of bright, steaming-hot lights blinding me. I'm not living my life."

"It's okay, Aunt Jan. We're all going to get through this. Right now, I think we should get up off the ground before one of the big rigs pulling in here runs over us. Here," he said jumping up and extending a hand to her, "let me help you up. Those police officers need to talk with you."

Jan slowly got up from the ground and leaned against Justin as they walked toward the barn. Someone reached out to steady her when she stumbled over the mat in front of Raven's empty stall. She looked up to stare into the troubled, blue eyes of a strange man wearing a black Stetson.

"Are you okay?" he asked . "Here sit down," he said offering her a canvas chair.

Jan ignored him and headed straight toward Lacey. She reached out and hugged her tightly. "I'm so sorry," she said. "I, I don't know where that came from. I didn't mean to hurt you like that. I know that you would never…".

"It's okay, Jan," said Lacey interrupting her. "How's your cheek?" she asked brushing Jan's unruly curls off her face. "I didn't mean to belt you like that, either." As the two women continued to stare at one another, Lacey suddenly started to laugh uncontrollably. The two of them just stood there clinging to each other giggling hysterically. The other's watched in total confusion.

"You two are crazy," announced Jamie with disgust. "We have a situation here—a serious one. Pull yourselves together for heaven's sake."

50

"Sorry, sorry," said Jan with tears rolling down her cheeks. "I know, I know," she said pulling away from Lacey and trying to regain control over her hysteria. "I just don't want to believe that Raven is really missing. Surely, he's around here somewhere. Surely," she repeated.

"I'm afraid he has been stolen, Miss Taylor."

"How do you know that, Mr. Kendall?" asked Jan. "You are Brett Kendall, right?"

"Yes. That's right. I'm Brett Kendall," he said offering his hand to Jan.

Jan hesitated for a moment and then shook his hand. "How do you know he's been stolen, Mr. Kendall?" she repeated.

"I recently fired one of my trainers, Phil Thompson, because he was dishonest. I discovered that he had been accused of falsifying breeding records and that he had actually been barred by AQHA from ever selling or training quarter horses."

"What does that have to do with Raven?" asked Jan impatiently. "Why would he steal Raven? How could that possibly be a way to get back at you for firing him?"

"He isn't trying to get even only with me," replied Brett. "I think he wants to get even with Jim too. Jim was the one who brought his record to my attention, and he knows how close Jim is to Lacey. That's probably why he went after Raven. He also realizes how valuable Raven is and how important he is to your breeding program."

"My god. What kind of man is this person? Is he likely to destroy Raven or to hurt him?" asked Jan sinking into a nearby chair.

"Honestly, I don't know He's not a good person.

I was going to fire him even before Jim came to me. He was cruel to some of the animals that resisted him, and I have no doubt that Raven put up a fight."

"Didn't anyone see or hear the ruckus?" asked Jan. "Surely, there was someone who saw him leading Raven out of here."

"That's what we are trying to find out," said one of the officers. "So far, we haven't found anyone who saw them take him from the barn or load him into a trailer."

"Them?" asked Jan. "What makes you think there was more than one person involved?"

"The footprints in the stall indicate two people— one wearing boots and another wearing athletic shoes. The boots were small, indicating it might have been a woman or a small man."

"I was walking around in the stall this morning," said Jan holding up her foot. "Here, see if these match the footprints in the stall."

The police officer gently removed the boot from Jan's foot and proceeded into the stall. "It does match the footprint," he announced as they all huddled around the stall door. "So, perhaps we are only looking for the person in athletic shoes."

"Phil always wore athletic shoes. He always complained about boots hurting his feet," said Brett.

"Great, just great," stormed Jan. "Where is this Phil Thompson now? Do you know where he might take Raven?"

Brett quietly shook his head and stared down at Jan. Her unkept, auburn curls were moving slightly in the soft, refreshing breeze that was blowing through the barn, and her tiny bare foot was sporting a beautiful pedicure. She was so small and delicate. *It's remarkable that a dainty, beautiful woman like she is can handle such an enormous, belligerent animal as Raven,* he thought. *Beneath her delicate exterior, I bet there is a determination that is stronger than that of any of the men I know. She could probably fight a tiger and win. I pity Philip if she ever catches him.* "I'm sorry. I don't know where he is, but I do have information about him that should help to track him down," he said. He reached out to touch Jan lightly on the shoulder. "I'm sorry you got dragged into my affairs."

Jan immediately jerked away from his reach and jumped up from the chair sending it flying backward against the stall. "Have you already given the police the information you do have?" she asked without looking at Brett. "Standing around here and waiting for someone to bring Raven back is not likely to solve my problem. We need to start somewhere, and this Philip jerk seems like a possible lead."

"What about you, Miss Taylor," asked the officer as he handed her boot to her. "Do you know anyone who might want to steal Raven? Do you have any stalkers or crazed fans we need to know about?"

"Everyone loves her," blurted out Jamie, coming up beside Jan and putting her arm around Jan's waist. "No one could possibly hate her."

Jan smiled at her niece's effort to protect her. "I haven't been famous that long to have stalkers and crazed fans threatening me," she responded, squeezing Jamie.

"What about insurance on Raven? Isn't he heavily insured?" asked the second officer.

"Of course, he's heavily insured," said Lacey, "but if you think we are purposefully hiding Raven, you couldn't be more wrong. Raven is more than a stud fee to us. He's part of this family. We're honest

53

ranchers who take good care of our animals," she stormed.

"There was a signed release form left at the stall office. The release was signed by you, Miss Taylor."

"It was obviously a forged signature. Believe me; I didn't sign any release form to have Raven taken off the grounds," shouted Jan.

"Isn't it true that the ranchers in your area have been having financial trouble," said the officer.

Brett immediately grabbed Jim Cordrey by the arm as he headed toward the officer with clenched fists.

"Don't you even think about accusing these women of any dishonest act," Jim yelled with his face so close to the officer that he backed up and immediately placed his hand on his tazer.

"Look, officers," said Brett. "Let's walk over to your cruiser, and let me tell you what I know about Philip Thompson. I know without a doubt that you are barking up the wrong tree here." Brett leaned his head slightly toward the door and stretched out his hand toward the cruiser, indicating that the officers should leave.

"Sorry, Miss Taylor," stammered one of the officers. "We're just doing our job. We will do everything we can to help you find your horse."

"Thanks," muttered Jan. "I appreciate that."

"We can't just sit and wait," shouted Justin as the three men walked toward the door.

"Where in the heck were you when all this was going on?" stormed Jamie. "Weren't you supposed to be cleaning out stalls in the next aisle? You couldn't possibly be finished with all of the stalls yet."

Justin looked away. "This isn't my fault," he said.

"Where were you?" insisted Jamie, stomping her foot on the ground.

"I went to breakfast with some friends," shouted Justin. "There, are you satisfied?"

"Whoa," said Jan. "It's okay. You're allowed to have some free time to spend with your friends, Justin. No one is blaming anyone for this. We have to stick together here instead of fighting."

"He's such a jerk," muttered Jamie.

"No he isn't," responded Jan. "He's your brother, and this wasn't his fault. We were out enjoying breakfast too. Remember? This is not our fault. It is the fault of some deceitful, hateful person, and if he or she does anything to hurt Raven, I swear I will tear whoever it is into tiny little pieces."

"Okay," said Jim. "Enough talk. Let's figure out what we can do. Brett has told me to stay here with the horses for the rest of the show. He's going to hire some security guards for his horses and for ours, I mean yours, but I'm going to take over one of the stalls for sleeping quarters."

"I don't want you to spend the next two weeks sleeping in the barn," said Lacey. "Any way, I don't think they'll let you do that. We'll take turns sitting in here at nights."

"Fine," said Justin, "but isn't all of this like *locking the barn door after the horse has bolted*? We need to find Raven today. Don't forget Jan starts showing the day after tomorrow."

"I'm afraid showing him this year is not an option," sighed Jan. "I just want to find him." Tears swelled in her eyes and rolled down her cheeks. "I just want him back," she whispered plopping down in the chair again. She pulled her knees up and hugged them tightly. "I had a dream..." she started. Suddenly, she stopped and jumped up from her chair. "Come on, Jamie and Justin, I think I know which way the trailer went that hauled Raven out of here. They can't have gone that far," she said running toward the truck. "Come on, you two. Now!" she screamed over her shoulder.

Chapter 7

As they were speeding down the road toward the hotel, Jan told Jamie and Justin about her dream and about the piercing scream from Raven that had awakened her. "I think the guy drove past the hotel on the way to the interstate. My bet is that he'll go south, probably heading for Mexico." As the hotel flew past them, Jan swerved around two cars and headed south on the freeway.

"He can't drive as fast hauling a trailer with Raven's weight behind him. We should be able to catch up with him, especially driving as fast as you are," said Justin. He leaned across Jamie to look at the speedometer, and they exchanged worried glances.

"There's no doubt we'll catch up with him at this rate, that is, if we don't get stopped by the police," added Jamie tightening her seat belt. "You'd better slow this thing down a little, Aunt Jan. We're about to go airborne."

Jan glanced over at the pale faces of her niece and nephew and laughed. "You two look scared to death. Haven't you ever driven ninety before?" she asked dropping the speed back to eighty.

"No," muttered Justin, "and now that I know how it feels, I don't think I ever will."

"Good," said Jan. "At least something worthwhile has come out of this mess. Sorry. I didn't mean to scare you. Jamie, you'd better call your mom and tell her what we're doing, but tell her not to call the police yet. If the jerk sees the police, he's likely to bail, and let the truck and trailer wreck with Raven inside."

As Jamie pulled her phone out of her jeans pocket, it started ringing. She glanced at the screen to see who it was. "It's Richard Evans," she said looking at Jan.

"Answer it, Sweetie, but don't talk too long."

"Hello, Richard."

"Thank goodness, I got you," said Richard. "Is your aunt with you?"

"Yes, she's right here. I'll put you on speaker, so she can hear you. She's driving like a Sprint-Cup race car driver, and I'd rather she not try to hold the phone."

"That's fine. Here's the deal. I'm following a truck hauling a horse trailer heading south on the interstate. I can't see the horse, but I can hear its piercing screams."

Jan looked over at the phone. "That has to be Raven," she shouted.

"I thought so," said Richard. "I heard the same scream go by the hotel just before Jamie came to tell me that he was missing. I remembered reading an interview of you in one of the horse magazines. You talked about his piercing screams. So, when they delivered your rental, I signed for it and took off. We just passed mile marker 124. Where are you?"

"I don't know. The mile markers are going by so fast that I can't read them," said Jamie glancing down at the speedometer that had started climbing back toward ninety. "For heaven's sake, Aunt Jan, slow this stupid rocket down," she screamed.

""Sorry," said Jan letting up on the accelerator. "We just got on the freeway, Richard, so we're at least fifty miles or more behind you."

"Okay. I'm going to cont nue to follow this jerk, and I'll keep in touch with you. Hopefully, my stupid cell phone holds out. I don't have a charger with me, and I'm bad about letting the battery go down. Also, I'm not sure how good the reception will be the farther we get from the city."

"If you leave the highway," shouted Jan, take the time to tie a rag on a fence post or road sign where we can see it. Do you have anything in the truck that you can tear up."

"I'll just tear up my shirt. It's red, so you should be able to see it."

"Great, now we're playing Hansel and Gretel," moaned Justin.

"Who was that?" asked Richard.

"It's no one," answered Jamie. "It's just my brother. We'd better hang up and save your phone. We can't thank you enough for what you're doing but be careful. Don't go heroic cn us if the guy stops. I understand he's not a nice person." She snapped the phone shut and smiled. "Well, what do you know about that? Richard's obviously a great guy."

"How do you know?" asked Justin. "Maybe he's in on the whole scheme, and he's just trying to find out where we are so he can throw us off."

"Impossible," said Jan. "His eyes are too kind."

"What? He has kind eyes?" blurted Justin disgustingly. "Just how do ycu tell that a person has kind eyes? What in the heck do kind eyes look like?"

"The opposite of yours," retorted Jamie.

"Come on, you two. Be nice. Let's talk about what we plan to do when we catch this jerk."

"At least we'll outnumber him," said Justin. "With

the help of this Richard hero, we should be able to hold him down long enough for the police to arrive."

"Good thinking," agreed Jan.

For the next few miles, they rode in silence. When the phone rang again they all jumped.

"It's Mom," said Jamie. "What do you want me to tell her?"

"The truth," answered Jan. "Put her on speaker, so I can talk to her."

"Hey, Mom," answered Jamie.

"Where are the three of you?" shouted Lacey. "I came back to the hotel, and the clerk said she hadn't seen any of you. Beth said she hadn't heard from you either. I hope your crazy aunt doesn't get you into some trouble that she can't handle."

"I can hear you," called Jan. "You're on speaker, so choose your words." She smiled as she heard the sigh from the other end of the phone.

"Where are you?" repeated Lacey.

Jan explained the situation to her and promised that they would not do anything stupid. "Just promise me that you won't call the police until I tell you to. I don't want to run the risk of this guy purposefully wrecking the trailer."

"I certainly appreciate you involving my two kids in all of this," scolded Lacey.

"We're fine," simultaneously yelled Jamie and Justin. "You worry too much, Mom," said Jamie. "We'll be just fine, especially if Aunt Jan can just keep this truck from flying."

"Jan, slow down," yelled Lacey. "I know how fast you drive. Do you hear me? You have my kids on-board."

"Got it." Jan laughed. "I'll keep you informed as soon as I know something."

"I'm going to call Jim and let him get hold of Brett Kendall," said Lacey.

"Don't you dare," yelled Jan. "I don't want Brett Kendall sticking his nose into any more of our business. Do you hear me?" When there was only silence from the other end, Jan cursed. "She already hung up, didn't she? Call her back, Jamie. Right now."

Jamie tried to reach her mother on the phone, but the call went straight into her mom's voice mail.

"I swear to goodness if those idiots do anything to cause this jerk hauling Raven to hurt him, I'll, I'll... Oh never mind," shouted Jan stomping on the accelerator.

Jamie and Justin exchanged looks and tightened their seatbelts another notch.

Chapter 8

Brett snapped his cell phone shut and grabbed his keys from the dresser in his hotel suite. He thought that Jan was probably right. Phil would head south with the horse. There was no way he could sell him in the states because Raven was too recognizable, especially by buyers who would be willing to pay the price that Phil was probably hoping to get out of him.

As he pealed out of the hotel garage, Brett hoped he could overtake Jan and the kids and get to Philip before they did. He was concerned about what would happen when they caught up with him. Philip always carried a gun, and he wouldn't hesitate to use it if he felt cornered. He had threatened Jim with the gun in the barn the day Brett had fired him. If he hadn't come up behind Philip and wrestled it away from him, he might have shot Jim. *I should have called the police then*, he lamented. *A good deed never goes unpunished—how many times do I have to learn that lesson?*

He headed his truck toward the heliport where his private helicopter was tethered. When he pulled into the heliport, Jim was already standing by the helicopter.

"How'd you get here so fast?" asked Brett.

"I flew. I ran at least two lights—doing a kind of stop, look, and go, rather than wait for the lights to turn," answered Jim. "Don't you think we should notify the highway patrol?"

"I don't know," said Brett. "That jerk will more than likely wreck the trailer on purpose if he thinks he can't get away."

"What makes you think that he'll do anything different when he realizes we've found him?"

"Hopefully, we can bargain with him—maybe offer him a chance to get away if he just gives us the horse."

"I don't mean to be critical, but you gave him a break a couple of weeks ago, and look what happened."

"I know," said Brett. "But I don't mind lying to him just to get my hands on that horse. We'll notify the police as soon as he turns over Raven."

"Don't you think he'll see through that?" asked Jim.

Brett motioned for Jim to climb into the helicopter. "Maybe, but maybe not. I didn't turn him in before, so he might just believe that I won't turn him in again."

"Well, I guess we don't have much choice. I agree. He won't think twice about flipping that trailer over or simply putting a bullet in Raven's head. He's vicious that way," yelled Jim above the roar of the rotors and engine of the helicopter.

Brett radioed the control tower and waited until he had authorization to take off. "Here we go," he said as the helicopter rose into the air and took off south following the interstate.

After a half an hour of staring at the cars below them, Jim yelled, "There's Jan and the kids. Man, she is flying as fast as we are."

"She won't be for long," said Brett, pointing to a

police cruiser racing up behind her.

"Yikes, that's going to be a big fine." Jim chuckled. He watched as Jan pulled the truck off the highway, and the cruiser pulled in behind it.

"Do you think we need to land out there in the field and go help her?" asked Brett.

"Nah," said Jim. "Jan can handle herself. I doubt that she'll even get a ticket. That woman can talk her way out of anything."

"She's quite a woman," said Brett.

"Yes, she is," agreed Jim. "I pity the poor guy who tries to tame her. She's a spitfire. I've never seen a horse she couldn't handle or met a man who could handle her. She scared both Robert and me to death, but she sure can sing. It's sometimes hard to believe that such an angelic voice could come from such a hell-cat." He laughed. Then noticing Brett's smile, he said, "Don't tell me you're interested in her?"

Brett chuckled. "She sure is easy to look at."

"So is Raven," said Jim, "but he would just as soon tear your head off as to let you touch him."

Brett burst out laughing. "Are you trying to discourage me?" he asked.

"Just consider yourself forewarned. You're a nice guy, and I'd hate to see you torn to pieces by the likes of Jan."

"What about you and Lacey, or am I treading on sacred ground there?" asked Brett.

"I've been in love with Lacey since the tenth grade, but she chose to marry my best friend. I can't help myself. I just keep thinking that eventually she'll get around to me. In the meantime, I don't mind waiting."

64

"Wow, now that's what I call unrequited love. You're a saint."

"Or a fool." Jim sighed and looked down at the highway below them.

For the next half-hour, they continued in silence. Brett couldn't stop thinking about Jan. Even with wet, uncombed, hair and red, puffy eyes full of tears, she was appealing. He had loved her CD's even before he realized that she was the girl next door, but he knew Jim was right about her. He could see the determination in her eyes, and it was obvious that she didn't care for him. He liked strong, independent women but wondered if he was up for the challenge that Jan Taylor would give him.

"Look," shouted Jim, interrupting Brett's thoughts. "There's the trailer."

"That's Philip all right, and that's my rig. That lousy jerk has stolen my rig to do his dirty work. Wait until I get my hands on him."

"What are we going to do now? Are you just going to let him see you?"

"Not yet. I've got a better idea. Get on the CB. Let's see if we can't get some truckers to help us out here."

"That's perfect. There's enough of them on the highway below us. If we can get them to box him in, we can land and hopefully get to him before he has a chance to do something stupid." Jim grabbed the CB mike and made an SOS call to truckers in the area. He asked for their help in corralling the horse trailer and forcing it off the highway at the next exit. "Be careful not to wreck the trailer," he warned the truckers. "It's carrying a valuable horse, and don't try to go near the horse if you don't want to be sent to the moon with two hoof prints on your butt," he added.

"Warn them that Philip might be armed," Brett added.

"My god, I never thought about that. I don't have a gun, do you?"

"Not on me. I left it in the truck. I was in such a hurry to take off that I didn't think to grab it. It's too late now to worry about that; just watch yourself when we get to him."

"Look," yelled Jim pointing to a group of truckers closing in around Philip's truck and the trailer. The truckers began to box him in on three sides, slowly moving closer and closer to the rig, squeezing it off the highway until Philip's only option was to go down the exit ramp. Another truck pulled across the bottom of the exit ramp, so there was no place for Philip to go.

Brett spotted a clearing and sat the helicopter down in the field next to the highway. He and Jim jumped out and ran toward the encircled rig. They knew they had only seconds to spare before Philip would get out of the truck and head for the trailer.

As Brett cleared the fence at the side of the field, he was shocked to see some young man jump out of a truck that had somehow been trapped between the horse trailer and the large tractor trailers. The young man was running toward the horse trailer. "Stay back," he shouted to the young man when he saw Philip jump out of the cabin of the truck with a gun in his hand.

Richard ducked as a bullet whizzed past his head. As Philip approached the end of the trailer, Richard tackled him and knocked him to the ground. By that time, Brett had reached them and managed to wrestle the gun away from Philip—but not before

66

he fired a shot. When Brett looked back, he saw Jim drop to the ground.

"You dirty, rotten coward,' Brett cursed at Philip. "It didn't have to end this way," he said slapping Philip on the side of the head with the butt of the gun. "Can you hold him down?" he asked of the young man lying on top of Philip.

"I've got this," yelled Richard.

Brett ran over to where Jim was laying motionless on the ground. Blood was oozing from a small wound on his shoulder, but his pulse was strong. In the background, Brett could hear sirens from approaching police cars. Obviously, the truckers had contacted them. When he looked back over to where Philip was spewing every curse word he knew and some that he seemed to be inventing, Brett noticed that two of the truckers were helping the young man get Philip up off the ground. Another trucker was heading toward Jim with a first-aid kit.

Jim opened his eyes and looked over at Brett. "What the heck happened?" he asked.

"He shot you. The stupid jerk shot you in the shoulder. Thank god it appears that he missed any vital parts."

The trucker began applying pressure to Jim's wound to stop the blood flowing from it. "It looks like the bullet went straight through," he said. "A few stitches and a bandage should fix you right up. I took a couple of bullets myself in Iraq. When they go straight through fatty tissue like this, you consider yourself a lucky man. In the army, we'd just stuff the hole with some gauze or anything that was semi-sterile and move on."

"Mr. Kindle," interrupted an approaching highway patrol officer. "We need to ask you some questions."

Brett and Jim looked at each other and chuckled. "I'm sure you do," answered Brett. "But first, can you call a squad for my friend here? And, how'd you know who I was, by the way?"

"The medics are already here," said the officer as two medics rushed over to Jim. "Jan Taylor told us who you were when I stopped her for speeding."

"Did you give her a ticket?" moaned Jim.

"A warning," said the patrol officer laughing. "She insisted that I didn't have the right to take the time to write her a ticket when there was a bigger crime being committed right under my nose. She promised to drive more cautiously if I would just stop the guy who had stolen her horse. She'll no doubt be wheeling in here in a few minutes. I didn't really buy her promise to obey the speed limit."

Brett smiled. "I'll be right back, Buddy," he whispered to Jim. He then turned to the trucker, "I don't know how to thank you guys. We couldn't have caught him without you."

"Things like this make our boring trips much more interesting," replied the trucker. "Glad we could help. I'll relay your thanks to the others."

"Thanks, again," Brett said lightly slapping the trucker on the shoulder. "You might tell them that they helped save Jan Taylor's horse."

"Really?" replied the trucker. "I love that gal's voice. Her CD was playing when you sent out the SOS. Well, now you have made my day," he said shaking Brett's hand so fast and squeezing it so hard that he thought he might crush it.

"Now, Mr. Kendall, if you'll just follow me, I need to have you tell me the details of what the heck is going on here," repeated the officer.

Brett climbed into the back seat of the patrol car, joining Richard, who was also sitting in the back of the cruiser. "Who are you?" asked Brett.

"Who are you?" replied Richard.

"I asked you first," insisted Brett.

"My name is Richard Evans. I'm a vet student who works nights at the hotel. I met Miss Taylor and her niece today when she arrived at the hotel."

"Vet student, huh?" replied Brett. "I'm Brett Kendall. I own the ranch west of the Taylor ranch."

"*The* Brett Kendall?" stammered Richard. "You're really the guy who owns half of the gulf coast and the most beautiful thoroughbred farm in Kentucky."

"Yes. I am that Brett Kendall. "Thanks for your help with this mess. If you hadn't stopped him, the jerk may have put a bullet in the horse's head."

"I wasn't expecting a shoot out," said Richard. "That first bullet just about parted my hair." He reached up and touched the top of his head to make sure once again that the bullet hadn't grazed his head. "What a day this has been for me—meeting both Jan Taylor and Brett Kendall."

Brett laughed and turned to glance out the window just in time to see Jan, Jamie, and Justin shoving past the security tape and heading straight for the horse trailer where Raven had begun to whinny wildly and kick at the tailgate. He stared in disbelief as Jan had Justin give her a leg up, so she could climb into the trailer. "My good god," he muttered beneath his breath. "That horse will crush her if she falls inside that trailer." He jumped out of the cruiser and ran toward the trailer yelling at Jan to

69

stay away.

Jamie grabbed him by the arm just as Jan leaped onto Raven's back. "Stand back. That's her baby in there," cried Jamie.

"She'll be crushed. He's out of control," insisted Brett.

"Raven would never hurt her. She'll have him calmed down in no time. Just be quiet and watch," Jamie ordered.

Brett and the others watched in amazement as Jan slowly slid on to Raven's arched back. Almost immediately, Raven's whinnies and screams turned to gentle nickers, and they could hear her softly singing to him. For several minutes, she lay on his back with her arms wrapped around his powerful neck, and no one in the on-looking crowd moved or uttered a sound.

"That lucky horse," whispered the police officer standing next to Brett.

Brett turned around and smiled. "I agree."

Chapter 9

After they had finally managed to get Raven back to the barn, Jan snuck off to the hotel. She wanted to be alone. The moment she closed the door to her room, she once again flopped across the hotel bed and grabbed a pillow to hug. Emotionally drained and physically exhausted she finally allowed herself to cry. Tears flowed uncontrollably down her cheeks, but this time they were tears of relief. Richard Evans and the show vet had given Raven a thorough examination. Other than a huge welt on his side, Raven appeared unaffected by his ordeal. Even with all the kicking in the trailer that he had done, the padded interior had prevented any visible injury to his feet and legs. *Thank god the jerk had enough sense to steal one of Brett Kendail's expensive rigs,* she sobbed.

She pondered about whether or not she should try to show Raven. He had to be tired, scared, and angry like her. He was an exceptional horse, and she knew he sensed things more than the other horses on the ranch. At least, he hadn't taken his anger out on her. He had responded immediately to her voice and touch in the trailer, but he had been even more reluctant than usual to allow Richard and the vet to examine him. If she hadn't been there to reassure him, they would never have been able to get near him without tranquilizing him. She wondered how he would respond to Jamie after she left to continue her tour. Perhaps she should just leave now and take him back to the ranch where they could be together a few days alone. But, there was the matter of titles and trophies. "Aaagh. I don't know. I don't know," she moaned pounding on the pillow.

The phone in her room rang, and she stared at it trying to decide if she should let it go unanswered. She knew that her family would call her on her cell phone, not the room phone. Finally, not able to tolerate the ringing, she reached over and grabbed the receiver. "Yes?" she answered impatiently.

For a moment, there was silence on the other end of the phone. *Whoever it was must have hung up*, she thought as she stared at the receiver.

"Miss Taylor, I'm sorry if I have disturbed you," said the caller finally. Jan immediately recognized the voice of Brett Kendall.

"What is it you want, Mr. Kendall?" she asked without trying to hide her annoyance.

"I was just checking to make sure you were all right. I heard that the vet checked Raven out and that he's fine," he responded. "He's an amazing animal."

Jan sighed. "Yes, he is. Other than the welt on his side, obviously put there by that idiot of a foreman you fired, he's fine."

"I apologize for that, but surely you know that I don't condone that type of treatment of animals."

"No, I don't know anything about your treatment of animals. The only thing I do know about you, Mr. Kendall, is that you collect them and that you also collect real estate."

Brett sighed. "Hmm, that's not an exact portrait of who I am. I'd like to give you the chance to know more about me. Would you consider having dinner with me?"

"Tonight? Are you kidding? I'm exhausted and want nothing to do with the world. All I want is peace and quiet and lots and lots of sleep. Good night, Mr. Kendall," she said slamming down the receiver. "Of all the nerve. How could he possibly imagine that I would want to have dinner with him. Geez he's arrogant." She pulled herself up from the bed and headed for the shower.

The warm, gentle spray from the shower slowly began to relax her tense muscles and ease her anger. This was one of the few things she liked in the world outside of the barn—a warm, soft, soapy shower. She sat down on the shower bench and let the light water spray wash away the horror of the day. She just sat there without thinking about anything but the pleasurable sensations from the warm water running over her body. Eventually, she began to feel guilty about all the water she was using, and she slowly reached out to turn off the shower.

She grabbed the thick, fluffy robe hanging next to the shower door and pulled it tightly around her. "Now to bed," she whispered aloud. As she flipped off the light and happily wriggled under the soft, down-filled spread, a rapid knock at her door startled her. "Go away," she called assuming it was Jamie or one of her sisters.

"Room service," called the shocked voice from the other side of the door.

"I didn't order room service," she groaned.

"It's a special delivery for you. I'll just leave it by your door."

"Wait. I'll let you in." She climbed out of the bed and peered through the security hole. She could see a young man holding on to a beautiful tray with a huge gardenia centerpiece in the middle of the cart. She loved gardenias. *It must be from Lacey,* she decided. *Why would she waste what money she does have on gardenias*, she wondered. "Sorry about that," she said opening the door. "I didn't mean to be so ill-mannered. I thought you were my niece."

"Where would you like me to put the cart?" the young man asked politely.

"Just put it over there by the table. Who sent it, do you know?"

"Sorry, I don't know. I was just told to deliver it."

Jan reached for her purse to give him a tip. "Please, that's not necessary," he said. "A generous tip has already been paid." He hesitated a moment by the door, then turned around quickly and blurted out, "I know this is not very professional, and I would probably lose my job if the management ever knew that I asked, but would you mind terribly signing my CD cover?" He whipped a copy of her latest CD out from under his jacket.

Jan laughed. "No, of course I wouldn't mind. I'm flattered that you asked."

"Make the autograph out to Melanie, if you would."

"Melanie?" asked Jan glancing up at the young waiter.

"She's my little cousin. They live in Little Rock. Her sister Jamie has cancer, and Melanie has sort of gotten lost in the shuffle since her parents have to spend all their time at the hospital with Jamie. She's coming to stay with us for the holidays. I know she's a great fan of yours, so I wanted to surprise her with this CD."

"Would her last name possibly be Kirby?"

"Yes it is. How do you know her?" asked the startled waiter.

"I met Melanie," said Jan amazed at how small

the world truly was. "She's a really sweet young lady. She was getting an autograph for her sister Jamie at my last concert. When is she coming here? I would love to do something special for her and for her family."

"She'll be here the day after tomorrow. This sure is a coincidence, isn't it? It's one of those serendipitous moments. Wow!" muttered the astonished waiter.

"The badge your wearing reads "David," is that your real name?"

"Yes. I'm David Kirby. Melanie is my cousin on our dad's side, so we have the same last name."

Jan recalled the note that Roger had given her with the Kirby's address in Arkansas. She could still see the sad look in Melanie's eyes when she had asked that the autograph be made out to her sister. "I'm giving a concert while I'm here. I'd love it if Melanie and you could be there."

"We'd love to come to one of your concerts, but…"

"I'll leave complimentary tickets and backstage passes for you at the door. How many tickets will you need?"

"Can I have eight? I don't mean to sound greedy, but I have three younger brothers and three sisters. They would be extremely mad if they couldn't come too."

Jan laughed. "Eight it is," she said. "You've made my day a whole lot better."

"Ditto," shouted David as he backed into the hall.

Jan closed the door and walked over to the serving cart. The gardenias filled the whole room with a beautiful, sweet aroma. Next to the gardenias, a bottle of her favorite wine was resting in a sterling bucket on top of a bed of round chunks of ice. She glanced around the tray looking for a card, but there was nothing to tell her who the tray was from. When she lifted the sterling dome from the plate, there was a succulent piece of prime rib perfectly cooked to her liking and a spray of roasted asparagus on the side. "This has to be from Lacey," she decided. "No one else knows my favorites like she does."

She reached for her cell phone and punched Lacey's number on speed dial. When Lacey answered, Jan could hear the noise of a crowd and some music in the background.

"Hello, Jan," shouted Lacey in the phone. "Where are you? You need to come out to the grounds. There's a big party going on."

"Why would I come out there when you sent me this beautiful supper tray with prime rib and wine to my room."

"What? What are you talking about? You know I couldn't afford to send you room service of prime rib and wine even if I wanted to, which I don't. We're chowing down on hot dogs and beer out here."

"Why aren't you at the hospital with Jim?"

"Because he's here with me. They treated him and released him after a couple of hours of observation. The bullet went straight through without hitting any major muscle or bones. A few stitches, some antibiotics, and they let him go. We're celebrating his good luck."

Jan shifted her gaze to the gardenias. "Well, I'm going to enjoy my prime rib even if I don't know where it came from."

"It's probably a gift from the hotel. Too bad I can't

sing for my supper," teased Lacey. "See you in the morning but not too early."

Jan was relieved that Jim would be okay, but she knew that he wouldn't be able to use his arm for several weeks. *Poor Lacey*, she thought. *This means that, once I'm gone, she and the kids won't have any help with the feeding or maintenance of the show barn for the two weeks they were planning to be here. This is a mess, and it's all Brett Kendall's fault.* She picked up her knife and stabbed at the thick, juicy cut of prime rib, then sliced off a small bite. "Oh my goodness, this is delicious. It practically melts in my mouth." She pulled the already loosened cork from the wine. "Here's to Raven," she said lifting her wine glass, "the one and only love of my life, now and forever."

Chapter 10

At five the next morning, Jan had already dressed and was about to text Jamie when she knocked at her door. "Good morning, Sunshine," said Jan giving her niece a quick hug.

"You're certainly chipper this morning," said Jamie. "Boy, it smells good in here. Where'd you get the gardenias?"

"Aren't they gorgeous? I'm surprised they haven't already turned brown. I have no idea where they came from, but they arrived last night with a wonderful dinner and a bottle of my favorite Merlot."

"Must be nice. I bet it was from the hotel, right?"

"Don't know; don't care, but I'm certainly grateful to whoever sent it. Let's get going. I'm dying to check on Raven."

"Justin, Richard, and I stayed with him until almost midnight," said Jamie. "I wanted to make sure he knew that I was there and that he could still trust me. Richard applied ice off and on for several hours to the welt on his side. We're lucky, the whip didn't break the skin, so it should be okay by the time I show him in the halter class."

Jan gave her niece another quick hug. "You're just like your aunt. Did you say that Richard stayed?" she asked. "Hmm. I bet it wasn't Raven *he* was concerned about."

"I certainly hope not," said Jamie beaming from

ear-to-ear. "He's everything I've ever wanted in a boyfriend—sensitive, smart, and a true animal lover."

"Not to mention exceedingly good looking," teased Jan.

"That's not as important as being a lover of animals, but it is a nice bonus," defended Jamie.

Jan grabbed the keys from the dresser and headed for the door. "Sure," she said turning around "his good looks are only a bonus." She laughed and ducked into the hall as her niece tossed a pillow at her.

When they arrived at the fairgrounds, Jan stopped outside of the barn and listened. "I don't hear Raven's wild screams. That's a good sign," she said. "Thank goodness." As they approached Raven's stall, she smiled when she saw Justin curled up on a bale of hay asleep in front of Raven's door. He had a horse blanket draped over him to keep warm. On the floor beside him, his iPod was plugged into a nearby outlet and playing a song from her latest album. "You kids are something else," said Jan. "I don't know what Raven and I would ever do without you."

When he heard her voice, Raven let out a loud whinny, and Justin jumped up, his eyes twirling in utter confusion and his fists clenched as if we was ready for a fight.

"Down boy," teased Jamie. "It's just us. Have you been here all night?"

"Good morning." Justin stretched and yawned. "Yeah, I must have fallen asleep after you and lover boy left."

"Don't start," warned Jamie. "I didn't tease you about the cute, young cowg rls that kept dropping by the stall all evening on the pretense of making sure Raven was okay."

"You may not have said anything, but you certainly did a lot of eyeball rolling and eyebrow raising," argued Justin.

"Whoa, you two. We're here to see if Raven is fit to show tomorrow, so cut out the silly nonsense and help me move this bale of hay out of the way."

Jan opened the stall door, and Raven rubbed his massive head against her jean jacket. She hugged him around the neck and reached up to kiss him on his huge cheek. "Good morning, fellow. You're such a toughie on the outside, but you're a real softie inside, aren't you?"

"Reminds me of you," said Jamie handing her Raven's lead line.

"Smart-alec," responded Jan pinching her niece on the cheek as she lead Raven out of his stall and headed outside to the exercise pens. As she worked Raven in the circle pen, Jan looked carefully for any evidence of soreness or lameness. "What do you guys think?" she called over her shoulder to Jamie and Justin.

"He looks fine," answered Brett Kendall, who was perched on the fence rail in the pen next to where she was working Raven.

Jan whirled around to stare at him. "I wasn't asking for your uninformed opinion," she snapped. "What do you think, Jamie? Do you see anything unusual about the way he's moving?"

"He looks great," answered Jamie, somewhat embarrassed by her aunt's dismissive attitude toward Mr. Kendall. "If anything, I think he's moving more consistently than usual."

"Go ahead, then, and you and Justin saddle up. I want to see how he does under-saddle. I don't think the welt on his side will be touched by the girth, but I

80

won't be able to tell if it bothers him until I ride."

Jan whistled for Raven, and he came to a sliding stop right in front of her. She reached up to rub his nose and muzzle and softly patted him on the neck. She pulled a peppermint from her jeans, and Raven waited impatiently for her to unwrap it. He quickly grabbed it when she placed it on the palm of her hand and offered it to him.

"Is that your secret for the excellent training you've done with him?" asked Brett. He hopped down from the fence and picked up Jan's work saddle that Justin had set on the ground.

"I can carry my own saddle, Mr. Kendall. I don't need any help."

"Are you ever going to stop calling me, 'Mr. Kendall'?"

"That's your name isn't it?" quipped Jan.

"My friend's call me Brett."

"Well, then I'll still call you, Mr. Kendall."

"Are you always this belligerent?"

"Only with people I don't trust," answered Jan. She snatched the saddle blanket from Brett's hand and tossed it on Raven's back. Brett started to lift the saddle for her, but she quickly grabbed it and easily placed it on top of the saddle blanket. Reaching under Raven's immense barrel, she grabbed the girth strap to tighten it. Keeping her hand on Raven as she walked behind him to the other side, she ran her hand gently down his side over the welt left from the whip. It didn't seem to bother him. Clutching the saddle horn, she easily swung up into the saddle without the use of the stirrups. She enjoyed Brett's startled look when she mounted from the left. "Don't look so startled, Mr. Kendall. I realize that you're supposed to mount from the right, but Raven has been trained to stand still no matter which side I choose to mount or dismount from."

"Don't you think you should walk him around a bit before you trust that the girth is going to stay tight?" Brett knew the moment that the words were out of his mouth that he was in for it.

"Please do me a big favor, Mr. Kendall, and mind your own business. Raven doesn't have any of the bad habits like swallowing air as do a lot of lesser well-trained animals." Jan clicked softly, and Raven immediately walked toward the rail.

"Way to go," whispered Justin as he rode past her. "Another arrogant male bites the dust."

Jan smiled at her nephew's approving comments. He obviously didn't care for the rich, handsome Mr. Kendall either.

"You were incredibly rude," said Jamie as she rode up next to Raven. "What's wrong with you anyway? He was just trying to be nice."

"He's insulting," countered Jan.

"Well, try to be polite. He's offered Richard a chance to intern with him next year. You know what that means, don't you?"

"It means her lover-boy will be next door," teased Justin. "Trust me. She isn't worried about Mr. Kendall's feelings one iota. Whenever she's nice to someone else, there's always something in it for her."

"You're a jerk," shouted Jamie.

"*Oh, it's a lovely day today,*" sang out Jan. "*So whatever you've got to do, you've got a lovely day to do it in, it's true.* Come on, you two, let's get serious here. Jamie, I want you to bring Brandy over and crowd Raven a little. I want him to get used to being bumped around a bit in the ring."

"Let Justin crowd him. I don't want him mad at me," protested Jamie.

"Oh for pete's-sake, one of you crowd us."

"I'll be glad to accommodate you," said Brett, riding his stallion close to Raven and bumping Jan's leg with his.

Jan was surprised to see how well he rode. "What will it take to make you disappear?" she said gathering the reins as she could feel Raven stiffen.

"Have dinner with me tonight, and I promise I'll disappear if you truly want me to after that."

"Fine. I'll have dinner with you. Just go away, and let me work my horse."

"Great. I'll pick you up at eight. I know a great Italian restaurant, unless you would prefer prime rib two nights in a row," called Brett as he rode away.

Jan stared after him with her mouth wide open.

"Big mistake," said Justin riding up beside her. "*Big* mistake." He intentionally bumped his horse into Raven causing him to break stride.

"Easy fellow," said Jan talking more to Justin than to Raven. "Do I detect a note of jealousy?"

"Jealousy? Of what? You're my aunt for heaven's sake. Mistrust, lots and lots of mistrust is what you should be detecting," he said as he galloped away.

"Well, look who has a new boyfriend now," mocked Jamie riding up beside her. "We've both won some pretty big prizes even before we've entered the show ring."

"I definitely don't consider the arrogant Mr. Kendall anything but a nuisance that I want to make disappear," snarled Jan.

"Yeah. Like heck you do." Jamie laughed and spurred her horse into a gallop to catch up with Justin.

Jan continued to work Raven, but her mind kept drifting toward the terrific dinner she had last night. *How in the heck would Brett Kendall know how I liked my prime rib cooked and that I liked my asparagus roasted? And the gardenias and wine… how could he know about them? Lacey! It had to be Lacey—no, wait a minute, it was Jim. It was certainly Jim. He's practically lived with us for years. Wait 'til I get my hands on him. Oh, my god, Jim knows everything about me.*

"Why are you galloping Raven?" yelled Justin. "Your mind better get back on the reason we're here. You have to win all of your classes, you know."

"Sorry," said Jan, embarrassed that her frustration and anger about Brett Kendall's snooping had caused her to squeeze Raven into a full gallop. She smiled at the disgusted look her nephew shot at her. "I'm back on track," she called out. "Watch me on reining pattern 5, and let me know what you think."

She jogged Raven over to the gate and turned him to face the center of the pen as if they were waiting to enter the show ring. On her command, Raven slowly walked into the ring. When they reached the middle of the arena, she stopped and settled him before beginning the pattern. He patiently awaited her cues before he moved. After several seconds, she kicked him off on the left lead to complete the first element that involved riding in three concentric circles of changing speed and size. He responded immediately to her subtle cues and

84

changed gaits smoothly. Between each subsequent maneuver, she stopped him, and he waited again for her to cue him before executing the next movement. As he executed the required 360 spinning turns, Raven planted his back, spinning foot and spun around so fast that the ends of the reins flew straight out, parallel to the ground, and his full, long tail flowed out from his body like it was being buffeted by the wind. Jan continued working through the pattern of slides, roll backs, and figure eights. Jamie and Justin watched with total admiration as Raven promptly responded to her slight squeeze to change his speed. His flying lead changes were so smooth that they were hardly noticeable unless you were watching for them.

Jan's favorite part of the pattern was the rollback that involved a sliding stop, a 180 degree turn, and a smooth lead off. She could feel Raven drop his hindquarters and plant his feet as they slid across the loose sand.

The final maneuver in reining competition is a sliding stop with an immediate back-up. Raven always seemed to enjoy racing forward at breakneck speed and then sliding along the sand to a complete stop before immediately digging in with his hind legs and pushing himself backward in quick, straight strides narrowly avoiding stepping on his beautiful, long tail as it dragged on the ground between his powerful hind quarters. Each movement was completed in one continuous, fluid motion with little or no evidence of Jan's leg pressure or rein movement. When Raven stopped, she leaned over and hugged him around the neck. "You are amazing, my mighty man," she whispered in his ear.

She was startled when she heard applause from the small crowd that had gathered around the pen. She and Raven had been lost in their own world, automatically performing the pattern as one, and everything else had just disappeared.

"Awesome," yelled Justin. "I sure wish he would work that way for me. You two are just plain amazing. Too bad you weren't being judged right now. You'd have taken first for sure."

"He never ceases to astound me," praised Jan. "He knows the pattern as well as I do and performs it perfectly, but he always waits for me to cue him and shows no sign of nervous anticipation of the different elements in the pattern. He could do it with anyone on his back."

"Oh no, he can't," countered Justin. "Just ask Jamie and Jim—we've all tried to work him through that pattern at the ranch. If he doesn't toss us off, we're lucky, and he acts like he has never performed the pattern in his life when we try to work him through it."

Jan laughed. "Sorry about that, but it's nice to know that he's a one girl guy and hopelessly devoted to me." Jan slid down on to the ground and tossed the reins over the saddle. Raven followed right beside her as she walked him around the ring to cool him down. When he became restless as the onlookers began to crowd close to them shoving autograph books at Jan as they headed out the gate, she finally had to grab the reins. "Sorry folks, let me get Raven brushed down and taken care of. Then, I can give out autographs. Please stand back. Raven doesn't like fans as much as I do," she said smiling at the young cowgirls wearing buttons with her picture on them.

For the next hour, she and Justin bathed and brushed Raven until his coat shone like a black diamond. The crowd of onlookers followed them to the washing bay and kept a silent distance while they dried and brushed him. Jamie had his stall cleaned and piled high with aromatic, cedar chips when they were finally finished with his grooming. She also had made sure that there was fresh water in his bucket and his favorite alfalfa in his feedbag.

When Jan led him into the stall, the first thing he did was lay down and roll in the cedar chips, completely undoing the work they had just done to keep his coat sparkling clean. Jan groaned. "That's Raven, for you. Okay, ladies " she said to the group of fans still gathered around the stall, "thanks for your patience. I have some time now to sign some autographs."

Jan was startled to see Jamie passing out signed photos of her. "Roger sent me a box of all kinds of give a-ways," she whispered to Jan.

That man never stops promoting me. I guess I should be grateful, thought Jan. "Thanks, sweetie. I didn't mean for you to have to be on *promotion duty.*"

"Actually, I won the coin toss this morning. Justin gets it tomorrow. It's fun. I don't mind it at all," said Jamie. "It makes me feel important."

Jan laughed. "You might not enjoy it so much when they start trying to pull out a lock of your hair or tear off the sleeve of your blouse."

"That actually has happened to you?" asked Jamie.

"Twice." Jan smiled at her niece's surprised look.

"Yikes. Maybe I should call Justin to get back here. He ran to the trailer to get a shower and spruce up before his lunch quest."

"Don't bother," said Jim Cordrey coming up from behind them. "I can fight off rowdy cowgirls even with one hand in a sling."

"I'm glad to see you're out and about after

yesterday's ordeal," said Jan, "but I have a bone to pick with you. What the heck have you told Brett Kendall about me besides my favorite meal, wine, and flowers?"

Jim laughed. "Hey. He's my boss. What was I supposed to do, lie to the man? He asked me about your likes and dislikes, and I told him, including the fact that you're a man eater."

"Do me a favor and keep your mouth shut. The less he knows about me the better I like it."

"I know a lot about him too," teased Jim. "Do you want me to tell you his favorites?"

"I'm not interested in learning anything about Mr. Kendall," said Jan snapping the end off the pen she was using to sign an autograph.

"Man, talking about him certainly makes you tense," said Jim handing her another pen. "Relax, will you? He's just a man."

"Shut up, Jim, and go away. I can handle my fans without any help."

For the next hour, Jan sat with Jamie in front of Raven's stall, signing autographs and talking to her fans who aspired to win at the World Show. The young women who hung around the stall seemed to have the same intense desire to show off their horses and their riding skills as she had. She enjoyed talking with people who shared the same passion that she had for horses. Although they knew she was a famous singer, they seemed more impressed with her achievements in the show ring.

The right to compete at the World Horse Show requires a lot of dedication and discipline. It takes time, money, and miles of travel to earn enough points at the various required state and national horse shows to qualify for the World Show. Points are awarded at the AQHA approved shows around the country based on the placement of the horse or rider in certain event classes. Riders have to prove that they are worthy competitors before they can show in the World Show. A horse is qualified to compete in each class in which it has earned the minimum number of points for that class. Points must be earned prior to August of each year for the November show. Although, there are no points awarded for participation in the World Show, any placing in the top ten, or as a Reserve World Champion or World Champion are recognized on the permanent record of the respective horse. Jan was proud of Raven's long list of world championships dating back to the time she entered him in his first halter class as a weanling.

The World Show is one of the biggest events in the horse industry. Each fall, the world's best American Quarter horses come to Oklahoma City to compete for the chance to win a share of the several million dollars doled out in cash and other prizes. For breeders like herself and Lacey, it was the most important time to sell their breeding program and to book their breeding appointments for the following year.

More than three thousand horses from all over the United States and the world compete for prizes in all types of events at the World Show. Raven's favorite event was reining, and Jan knew that he just tolerated the other competitions for her sake. The reining event allowed Raven to show his versatility in speed, agility, and suppleness.

After the autograph session, Jan helped Jamie and Justin clean the other stalls, lunge some of the other horses, and polish the silver on their show halters and saddles. Working in the barn helped Jan to feel like herself again. Financial and touring woes vanished in the emptied wheelbarrows of manure and soiled cedar. She was surprised when Jamie told her it was five o'clock. "Wow, the time has just flown by," said Jan. "I can't believe it's five already."

"You'd better head back to the hotel and get ready for your hot date," teased Jamie.

"She'd be better off to stay here," said Justin tossing the silver polishing rag across the room. "I don't get it. He's obviously not your type. Why would you bother giving him the time of day, let alone agreeing to have dinner with him?"

Jan sat down next to Justin on the bale of straw and put her arm around him. "You know," she said, "I have no idea why I said I'd go other than he promised that he'd disappear if I'd just have dinner with him."

"Just don't let him talk you into selling any more of the ranch," grumbled Justin.

"Aha, so that's why you don't like him. You don't have to worry, my little nephew. I would never agree to sell him even a blade of grass. Anyway, your mom has the final say over stuff like that, not me."

"But you can stop her, can't you? She's not like you. She doesn't like horses the way you do, and Aunt Beth doesn't care two hoots about horses or the ranch. It scares me to think that mom might just up and sell it. I know she's worried about my college tuition and about Jamie's vet school tuition if she actually gets accepted."

"I'll get accepted; don't you worry," retorted Jamie.

"That's not the point," said Justin. "What good will it do for you to specialize in large animals if we lose the ranch?"

"Don't you two worry. I'll have a talk with your mom. We're not going to sell the ranch, and you're college tuition will be paid for, even if it means I have to tour around the country forever," Jan promised.

She was saddened by the sudden realization that her niece and nephew were worried about finances and their future, but it just proved to her how much more sophisticated they were than most kids their age. "Justin, I promise that the wealthy Mr. Kendall will never buy the ranch, but there's an old saying, '*keep you friends close and your enemies closer*, and that's the strategy I plan to pursue with our Mr. Moneybags. Okay?"

"Fine," muttered Justin. "You'd better get going, but don't spend too much time getting glamorous for him. I can see the way he looks at you."

Jan laughed and leaned over to give her nephew a quick kiss. "You're as perceptive as Raven, and you two are the only men I have time for in my life."

Chapter 11

Jan glanced once more in the full-length mirror on the closet door in her hotel room. She had dressed casually for her date with Brett Kendall, wearing a full-length jeans skirt tastefully split up the front to show off her new Tony Loma western boots. Her crystal decorated, green peasant blouse matched her eyes, and the neckline was appropriately seductive. She finished inserting the large-hoop silver earrings through her ears and smoothed her hair that she had pulled back and gathered into a French knot at the base of her neck. Spotting the beautiful gardenias, she carefully pulled out one of the small ones and tucked it on one side of the French knot. She grabbed her small, denim clutch bag then headed down to the hotel lobby where she was to meet Mr. Kendall. She smiled as she realized she still used his formal name even in her thoughts about him.

As she exited the lobby elevator, Brett jumped up from the sofa where he had been waiting for her. He obviously wasn't prepared for the swarm of fans that nearly knocked him over to get to her. Jan noticed the startled look on his face as her young admirers jostled him aside, but when one of the girls grabbed the gardenia from her hair, he immediately shoved his way through the crowd and grabbed her possessively by the arm bellowing at the fans to move back. Richard also came to her rescue pushing and shoving the crowd away while Brett led her to his awaiting Escalade. Once inside the car, she tried to reassemble her disheveled hair. She finally gave up on the French knot and shook her hair loose so that it fell around her shoulders.

"My good god. Does that happen to you often?" Brett asked as he shoved the arm of an insistent autograph seeker away and quickly closed the door. "Are you okay?" He turned to look at her and slipped his arm around the back of her seat, barely touching her shoulders.

Jan knew he was genuinely concerned, and she was too. "I don't usually go out without a disguise or a security guard. I let my niece and nephew talk me out of wearing my new blonde wig, not that the disguise always works."

"I had no idea about the threat to your safety, or I would never have asked you to meet me in the lobby. The girls at the World Show were so much more respectful this morning. These people were more wild and determined to grab a piece of you. I'm so sorry."

"It's not your fault, but it's one thing I don't like about my singing career. I think it's because I'm the new kid on the block that they're so persistent. I understand that the packs of admirers will begin to diminish when a new star surfaces to take my place."

"Do you think we should risk going to the restaurant?" asked Brett.

"You didn't tell them when you made reservations that I was dining with you, did you?"

"No, of course not, but there's a string of cars packed full of people lined up behind us," he responded. He reached up to adjust his rear mirror and frowned at the number of fans piling into the cars parked along the street. "I don't relish trying to fight them off during what I hoped would be a quiet dinner with just the two of us."

"Well, let's just see how good your evasion skills

are, Mr. Kendall. I know your spying skills are good; let's just see how great your driving prowess is and how quickly you can lose them."

"Fasten your seat belt, young lady. I used to drive in the dirt track races all across Tennessee and Kentucky," bragged Brett, "but I'm not leaving this spot until you promise to stop calling me Mr. Kendall." He jumped as one of Jan's admirers loudly pounded on the passenger window, and Jan's head jerked back against the headrest as he sped away from the curb.

She braced herself against the seat as he stealthily dodged in and out of traffic and slid around a corner practically on two wheels through an amber traffic light. "Maybe I would be safer in the middle of the mob. I think that last turn lost most of them but a couple of the diehards. I'm impressed. You drive faster and more reckless than I do."

"I'm not so sure about the faster part. I saw you speeding down the highway yesterday from the helicopter. Hang on," he warned as he flipped around another corner. "There, I think that should do it." He glanced over and smiled at her. "Are you still with me?" he asked. "You look a little queasy."

"Well, let's just say that you've pushed my vertigo to its limit. I thought I was reckless, but you're insane."

Brett tossed his head back in a hearty laugh and reached over to squeeze her clammy hand. "I'm sorry. That just proves how much I want to spend a night alone with you."

"We're spending a meal with each other, not a night," she said sarcastically. "Let's just get that straight. I don't do 'one nighters'—never have, never will."

"Don't flatter yourself. It was just a phrase, not an invitation," he retorted. "You're absolutely the most irritating person I have ever met. You treat your horse better than you treat most people."

"Of course, I do. I can trust Raven." She could tell by Brett's slumping posture that she had further irritated him. They rode in silence until they finally reached the restaurant. "I'm sorry if I offended you, *Brett*," she said intentionally emphasizing his first name.

"Well now, that's a start.' Brett opened his door, and when he saw her reach for the door handle on her side, he said, "Would you mind just staying put for a second, and giving me a chance to open your door? Southern gentlemen still prefer to practice chivalry."

"Sorry," muttered Jan feeling appropriately chagrined.

The maitre de greeted Brett by name and led them to an isolated booth hidden from the view of the other patrons by a sheer fabric enclosure. "This is cozy," muttered Jan, smiling warmly up at Brett. *My goodness, he is handsome,* she thought. She was startled by the sudden rush of pleasure that engulfed her body. *I guess I never seriously looked at him before. Beth is right, his eyes could penetrate a steel door, but there's a softness in them too. Whoa, girl, don't forget that you don't like him. He's the enemy, not the friend,* she reminded herself.

"Would you like another Merlot or do you prefer a different wine with pasta?" asked Brett, interrupting her thoughts. "I forgot to ask Jim about that," he teased.

"I warned Jim not to give out any more of my secrets. He knows me as well as my sisters know me. He's a great guy, but he obviously talks too much."

95

Brett laughed. "I promise that from now on I will get my information from the original source. That is, provided I'm not ordered to disappear after tonight."

"As long as you don't try to tell me how to ride my horse or try to purchase a single inch of my property, I won't ask you to disappear."

"Look, Jan. Let's get one thing straight. I am not the land-grabbing, merciless real estate tycoon that you and Justin think I am. I honestly have purchased land only to keep the ranches in central Texas from being sold to developers. I don't mean to indicate that I don't have selfish intentions for helping the other ranchers, because I do. I don't want my ranch to be surrounded with country-club homesteaders living on five or ten acre plots like is happening in Kentucky. I want to preserve the Texas wide-open range if that's at all possible."

"So do I," said Jan, stunned at Brett's obvious passion for the preservation of ranching. "How did you know about Justin's feelings for you?"

"He's pretty transparent," said Brett. "I admire the boy and hope eventually to win his trust. Jim is always telling me what a natural seat he has in the saddle and about his ardent interest in ranching."

"He's scared that his mom will sell her share of the ranch. I know that Lacey has a lot on her plate both financially and personally. Those kids are her life, and I know that she would sell anything she had to ensure that they both get the education she wants them to get. I only wish I could kick in more. If it hadn't been for this stupid tour ..." she stopped, realizing she was disclosing more than she wanted Brett to know about her.

Brett obviously could tell that she didn't want to continue the conversation about her personal business. She was glad that he didn't pursue her comment about the tour. Instead, he tactfully covered her discomfort by lifting the bottle of wine and filling her glass, then his. He raised his glass toward her and offered a toast, "Here's to Texas, horses, and us, hopefully not always in that order."

Jan smiled, noting his reference "to us" and willingly touched her glass to his.

Chapter 12

Jan was up before dawn. It was their first day of showing, and she wanted to turn Raven out in the outside arena before others started lining up to work their horses. She knew that a little time for him to run, buck, and jump would help to settle him before he had to perform. She sent Jamie a text saying that she would meet her at Fair Park later and slipped down the back stairs of the hotel. She didn't want to take the risk of running into a horde of fans by exiting through the main entrance. Experience had taught her that some of them never seem to sleep. She had phoned Richard at the front desk, and he agreed to meet her in the back stairwell to walk her to her truck.

"Good morning," said Richard as she arrived at the bottom of the twelve flights of stairs. "You're wise to slip out the back way. Even though we forced your fans to leave the lobby, several of them are parked outside the front entrance. We called the police, and they threatened to arrest them for loitering, but they just keep coming back. That sucks. You should have security with you all the time."

"What's Jamie doing up so early, and who's that with her?" asked Jan as she watched Jamie pull the truck over to the curb and a uniformed security guard jump out of it.

"I called her. The hotel has taken on some extra security after last night's fracas. I had one of them walk down with Jamie to get the truck for you. I'm serious. You shouldn't be running around in the wee small hours of the morning by yourself. Justin and Jim are going to meet you at the stall. I'd go with you, but I have to study and get to class this morning."

"For heaven's sake. I really have become a liability, haven't I? I bet my family and the hotel will be glad to see me and my tour bus leave." Jan gave him a quick hug and climbed into the truck.

Richard walked over to the driver's side and leaned in to give Jamie a quick kiss on the cheek. "Be careful, and call me if you need anything."

"Hey, the family has this covered," Jamie said, flashing him a grateful smile and a sexy wink.

As they pulled out of the driveway, Jamie glanced in the rear-view mirror. "Hmm, the paparazzi never give up, do they? You are just too famous for your britches," she said reaching out to grab Jan's hand.

Jan glanced in the side mirror at the car that fell in behind them as they exited the garage. "I recognize that one. He's a photographer that shows up everywhere snapping pictures that he sells to the tabloids. He's harmless—he's just trying to earn a living. He's actually helped Roger out with security a couple of times."

"Speaking of Roger, mom called him last night and told him about the mob in the hotel. He'll be here this afternoon."

"Aagh," moaned Jan. "I'm so sorry to be such a nuisance."

"Stop that. You're not a nuisance. This is all kind of exciting for all of us normal folks who live quiet, mundane lives isolated from the rest of the world on thousand acre ranches in the middle of nowhere."

"You have no idea how much I wish I could still lead such a mundane existence. Not that I'm not grateful to the fans who buy my CDs; I am. Most of them are like the ones we saw yesterday—calm and genuinely interested in me as a person, not as a trophy on their bedroom wall. It just takes a few obsessive nuts to make your life miserable and tarnish the pleasure."

"Oh, the price of fame and fortune," teased Jamie. "Forget it and put everything out of your mind, including Brett Kendall. By the way, how did that go last night? She turned and glanced sideways at Jan, then burst out laughing. "You fell for him, didn't you? I knew you would."

"I wouldn't exactly say I 'fell for him', but we did have a delightful dinner, after which he snuck me up the back stairs to my room, and immediately left after a very warm, lingering good-night kiss."

"Yes, yes, yes! I love it. My man-eating aunt is falling in love."

"Don't exaggerate, Jamie. I enjoyed being with him, that's all. I doubt that anything will ever come of it. Come on, let's not talk about Brett. We've got bigger fish to fry today. My cutting class is first up this morning, and our team pen is this afternoon.

"So it's Brett, now, instead of Mr. Kendall."

"I'm not kidding, Jamie. Focus."

"OK, OK. For starters let's talk about the team pen. Jim still insists that he can ride with one hand, but I'm not sure."

"He could ride with no hands. That horse of his is so broke that a baby could ride it."

As they pulled into the parking lot beside their show barn, Jan was startled to see five or six trucks already there. "Jeez. What time is it?" she asked. "I thought we'd be the only ones out at this hour."

"Texan ranchers stick together, don't you know that by now? Mom called in the cavalry last night. We have around the clock security for our horses and for you—all free of charge."

"What?" screeched Jan. "You're kidding, right?"

"Nope," said Jamie. "Bill Fletcher and his family drove all night to get here, but most of the other ranchers already had someone here. When they heard about Raven's abduction and the mob scene in the hotel, they all volunteered to send someone from their ranch to help us out. They've agreed to take turns monitoring the barn and every show you're in."

Tears welled in Jan's eyes. "You've got to love Texans," she whispered. As she got out of the truck, she recognized several of the ranchers from her hometown leaning against the outside pen.

"Howdy, Jan," said Bill Fletcher from the Split Rail Ranch that borders their ranch on the south. "Heard you needed some help holding off some of those fans of yours."

"I don't know what to say. Y'all are certainly a welcomed sight." One by one she hugged each of the five volunteers. "I sure miss seeing y'all at the Grange back home," she said.

"We sure miss your singing too. You going to be back for the holiday dance?" asked Bill.

"I sure will. I can't thank y'all enough and apologize for being such a nuisance. I'll be out of here in a couple of days, I promise."

"Heck, no hurry," said Bill. My wife has been wanting to come to this show for years. So, here we are. Don't you worry that pretty little red head of yours about us. We're just going to get out of your way and let you get to work."

A flash went off behind her, and Bill and the other ranchers took off sending the young photographer running for his car. "He's harmless," shouted Jan. She laughed as she headed inside to get Raven. "Our next problem will be to keep them from turning into vigilantes," she said hugging Jamie around the waist as they walked through the barn.

Justin and Brett were already standing by Raven's stall, and Jan was relieved to see that they seemed to be having a civil conversation. "What are you two doing here so early?" she asked smiling up at Brett.

"Spying on my competition for the cutting class," he said. "You'll be glad to know that Justin and I have decided to bury the hatchet and concentrate on your security, but don't expect me to be lenient with you in the show ring. I can already see that cutting trophy in my trophy room," he teased.

"We'll just see about that," said Justin slapping Brett on the shoulder as he handed Raven's lunge rope to Jan.

Jan smiled and opened Raven's stall. "Hey, buddy, how's my best man today?"

"Humph," said Brett clearing his throat.

"Give it up, man," said Justin. "You'll never be ranked above Raven, believe me; I know that for a fact."

Jan led Raven to the exercise pen and then turned him loose. She climbed up on the fence rail next to Brett to watch him play. The brisk November breeze blew her hair and sent a shiver through her. She pulled the collar of her jeans jacket up more closely around her neck and hugged herself.

"You cold?" asked Brett reaching out and pulling her closer to him.

102

She could feel the warmth of his body as she leaned against him. "I'm okay," she muttered.

"I had a good time last night," he whispered through her hair.

"Me too." She turned around and smiled up at Brett, brushing her hair back from her face, so she could see him better in the light of the early dawn.

"Any chance of a repeat tonight? I know a quiet Mexican Restaurant." He smiled down at her and gently kissed her on the tip of her nose.

She hesitated before answering him, wanting desperately to say 'yes' but knowing that she couldn't. "I'm sorry, Brett, but starting today, I'm going to be tied up with showing. Then my band arrives tomorrow, and I have to rehearse for the Friday night show. I pull out of here right after my performance to head to Albuquerque for a Saturday night concert." Jan could feel the return of the cold as Brett pulled his arm from around her waist, and she felt his body stiffen. Trying to change the conversation she said, "I was glad to see you and Justin together this morning. How'd that happen?"

Brett was quiet for a moment, then finally heaved a sigh and answered, "After I dropped you off at the hotel, I came back to the barn to check on my horses and saw him sitting outside of Raven's stall. I sat down and had a man-to-man talk with him. He's a good kid, and there's no doubt that he would fight a buzz saw for you and your family."

Jan smiled. "He's my rock. He keeps me calm. He's so much more sophisticated than most college freshman. I know he'll be a great rancher and a solid family man. Some girl would be lucky to catch him."

"He misses you. He's worried that you're not happy touring the country, even though you love to sing. Are you? Happy, I mean?"

"I'm happier when I'm back at the ranch, but I've got contracts and other commitments that will keep me from staying home much the next couple of years. Then, hopefully, I'll be able to come home and stay around longer."

"Hmm," said Brett as he jumped down from the fence. "Well, then, I guess I'd better let you get on with what you have to do. It doesn't sound like there's a spot for me in your crowded schedule."

"Brett," she called, but he walked toward the barn without looking back. Raven came to the fence and nuzzled her as if he sensed that she needed him. "Hey, big fellow, you'll never just walk away from me will you?" she whispered as a single tear trickled down her cheek and fell into Raven's thick forelock. She slid off the fence on to Raven's broad back and grabbed hold of his mane. She let the chilly November breeze blow through her hair and her heart as she raced him around the arena, both of them free from any attachments except for one another.

Chapter 13

The rest of the morning passed in a flurry of preparations for everyone's show schedule. Jan, Jamie, and Justin were all showing in several different classes, so there was constant activity in the barn as they readied their various horses for each class. Jamie kept everything orderly in the tack rooms by yelling at anyone who didn't put a piece of tack back in the right place.

Lacey wasn't showing, so she was the orchestrator of the whole chaotic scene and made sure that everyone had the right number for the right event and arrived on time for their classes. AQHA rules and regulations clearly state that a horse could be disqualified should the exhibitor cause any unnecessary delay in bringing the horse into the ring, so timing and organization in the barn were critical. Given their push for Raven to win the All Around again, there could be no mishaps in the scheduling resulting in a potential disqualification.

~~~~~

Jan and Raven waited outside for their entrance into the arena for the cutting class. She didn't like to watch her competition perform because it made her more nervous. She glanced around looking for Brett and spotted him sitting nonchalantly on this horse talking with a group of the other riders. He had his back to her, and she wondered if that was intentional. *Forget about him*, she thought. *It wasn't meant to be. Just concentrate on getting Raven his championship. That's what matters at the moment.*

When her number was called, she heard the announcer remind the audience of the need for quiet during the class to avoid possible injury to the rider, horse, or cattle. Although he didn't mention her by name, she knew that he was trying to protect the opportunity for her and for Raven to perform without distraction. When she walked Raven through the gate, she glanced up at the seats in the arena. It was full of people. Some were holding up signs that read, *We love you, Jan.* She drew in a deep breath and prayed they would respect the announcer's request for silence. She leaned forward and patted Raven on the neck. "OK, fellow," she whispered. "Here we go. It's just you and me now."

As if he understood, Raven tossed his head and lightly pawed the ground. When they entered the working area of the arena, Raven went straight to work. He expertly cut his first calf deep from the herd without any disturbance to the other calves. He easily moved the calf to the center of the arena and began to strategically keep it from returning to the herd. He continued to work it at a sufficient distance to keep from upsetting the others, and then let it loose, so he could cut out another calf. Jan kept her reins loose and avoided any cueing of Raven to allow him to work the cows alone to demonstrate his savvy prowess in the short two and a half minute time limit for the performance. It was like poetry in motion to watch the game between Raven and the calves. Jan stayed perfectly balanced in the saddle as Raven jumped quickly back and forth working with the calf.

When they finished their run, the crowd went wild. Jan tipped her hat to them and rode out of the arena. As she headed out the gate, Brett was waiting to enter. "Nice work," he said casually, as if he were talking to any competitor. "I'm not sure anyone could beat that performance, but I sure intend to try."

She saw him heave a sigh and shoot her a disgusted look when the ring steward asked him to wait until the large crowd that was exiting had time to

106

clear the arena, so his horse wouldn't be distracted by the noise and movement.

She tried to move outside of the arena before the crowd began to rush toward her. Out of nowhere her Texan security guards appeared. They quickly surrounded her and kept the crowd back.

"Sorry, folks," she shouted above their noise. "I'm a working cowgirl today, not a country star, so please let me do my job here. Please. I will have an autograph signing at noon in the Cafe, but until then, I'd surely appreciate your cooperation if you'd not interrupt Raven's performances."

She slid off Raven, who was becoming agitated by the waving signs and shouts from her fans. She put her hand under his chin to pull his head next to hers. "Easy, baby," she whispered. "It's okay."

"You and Raven are simply awesome," said Bill Fletcher as he fell in beside her to hold back the persistent autograph seekers. "He's such an imposing animal but so gentle when it comes to working the calves. I'd give anything if my horse could work like that. You've got the win sewed up. No one could match the two of you."

"I hope you're right," answered Jan. "But there are a lot of good horses left to work. I couldn't hear my scores above the roar of the crowd. Did you hear them?"

"Yeah, I did hear them. You got three seventy nines, a seventy-eight and a perfect eighty. That's a 237 out of the possible 240 after they toss out the highest and lowest scores. I think you should have had all eighty's myself. I didn't see either you or Raven make a fault on any of his cuts."

"You're prejudiced," said Jan reaching out and giving his hand a squeeze.

She wanted to wait and watch Brett ride, but she didn't. When they finally made their way back to the barn, Jamie and Lacey ran to meet her. "You were awesome, Aunt Jan. Just plain awesome," chattered Jamie.

"I'm just glad that's over," said Jan. "One down, three more to go," she muttered as she slid the saddle off Raven.

"I'll rub him down," said Jamie. "Why don't you go and grab something to eat. I know you didn't eat this morning."

"You've got plenty of time before the next go-round, if there is one." said Lacey. "Why don't you go over and see Beth at the Cox Pavilion. You haven't seen her since the other morning."

"Right. I'll go by Beth's first. I want to check out her paintings and warn her that Roger will be here today," replied Jan.

"She knows," said Jamie. "She was the one who insisted that mom call him. She was furious that he hadn't provided you with any security while you were here."

"I guess I'd better tell her that he offered, but I refused. I've never had any problems here before."

"You weren't as well known before. Now, you're a star and everyone wants a piece of you," replied Lacey.

"Stardom is not all it's cut out to be," she called back over her shoulder as she stuffed her hair under the blonde wig and slipped on her large sunglasses. As she left the stall area, she noticed that Tim Fletcher, the oldest son of Bill Fletcher, fell in behind her. "Poor guy, he looks like he would rather be doing anything but following me around," she muttered under her breath. "This sucks for both of us."

108

Beth was sitting in front of a huge easel with her back to a small crowd of onlookers who were enthralled at her ability to transform a glob of paint into stunning clump of trees on a hillside.

"Hey, Sis," called Jan.

"Hey, stranger. Nice wig and sunglasses," said Beth pulling over a stool for Jan to sit down next to her. "I hear you've had quite an exciting last couple of days. You should take up painting; it's safer." She laid down her brush and leaned over to give Jan a hug. "You don't look very happy, sweetheart. What's wrong?"

"Nothing's wrong—at least not for the moment. Raven performed like the winner he is during the cutting class." Jan got up and moved closer to a large western painting that caught her eye. "Your new paintings are gorgeous," she said.

As she carefully examined the faces on the cowboys in Beth's paintings hanging on the booth walls, she was immediately aware of what Lacey was talking about earlier. Every single face was Roger's.

"Don't tell me. I already know. My cowboy's look like Roger," said Beth turning around to face her. "I guess I can't get him out of my mind. I don't know what to do."

She looked so sad that Jan reached out and embraced her. "Sweetheart, he feels the same way you do. He loves you, and I can assure you that he's clean—no drugs, no alcohol for more than a year, and he never even looks at other women. He's going to be here in a couple of hours. Are you going to give him another chance?"

"I don't know, Jan. I'm afraid of winding up in the same place we did last time. He's still going to be gone a lot, and you know how I hate to travel."

"Well then, stay home. He won't care if you don't join us on the road. I know he won't—just as long as he can come home to you whenever he can."

Beth reached up to straighten a painting hanging on the wall of her booth. "What kind of life is that?" she asked.

"It's the way everyone lives in the music industry. Anyway, you like being alone, for god's sake. You never come out of your studio at home unless we drag you out. But, you don't have to shut him out. He loves you."

"I don't know; I just don't know. I'm okay the way I am," insisted Beth.

"Are you willing to settle for just being okay? Come on, Beth. There's more to life than painting—much more."

"You're a good one to talk," accused Beth. "You scare every man away before he even has a chance to find out if he loves you. You're going to be thirty-three in a month. Don't you want to fall in love and have kids?"

"You're right. I'm not the best role model in the world, but my situation is a lot different. I have contracts to meet and a band to support. I'm never in a city longer than 24 hours. My career is different. I have to bounce around the country right now; you don't."

"And how is all that working out for you? You look like hell with your droopy, down-in-the mouth look. I have yet to see you smile since you've been here."

Jan was startled at Beth's description of her. "Well, things haven't been going all that well the past two days as you're certainly aware, but I smiled last night," she dropped her eyes and looked off in the distance. "Actually, I smiled a lot last night. I even laughed," she muttered as she plopped back down on the stool.

"I heard you went out with the awesome Brett Kendall. Tell me all about it," said Beth suddenly super-charged.

"Sorry, there's not much to tell. We had a wonderful time last night, and he walked away this morning." She was surprised at the swelling of tears that threatened to spill over on to her new show shirt.

"Why? It couldn't be that he didn't like you. You're gorgeous, talented, and very, very loveable," said Beth reaching out to take Jan's hand.

"You just said I looked like hell."

"You do right now, but I'm sure you didn't look like that last night. I bet you told him that you were too busy to go out with him, right?"

Jan looked up at Beth.

"I knew it; I knew it. Why can't you just relax this week and have some fun? You don't have to be in that barn all the time. Like right now—you should be over at the Café having lunch with him. Go and get out of here. Find him and show him a little interest."

"I really can't, Beth. I really can't start a relationship with anyone right now. I'm okay; really I am. Who knows, maybe in a year or two I'll look him up, and we can start again."

"Now listen to who's settling for 'okay'. Look, Jan, guys like that don't come around very often. Once burned, they stay that way. If you don't leap now, you may as well kiss your chances with him good-bye."

Jan put her hands to her lips and threw a kiss to the wind. "Good bye, Mr. Kendall," she whispered. "Well, got to go, Sis. I have to sign autographs for a while at the Café and then get over to the barn for the Team Pen event. Jim's going to ride with one arm in a sling. Hope it works. Raven needs the points."

"Always what Raven needs—what about your needs, Jan? Take my advice, hook up with Brett Kendall."

"And you take mine—give Roger another chance." Jan turned around and winked. "Love ya," she called as she linked arms with Tim Fletcher "How'd you like to have some lunch with me, Tim, while I sign a few autographs."

"Love to, Miss Taylor," he said. "It'd be a real pleasure. But, if I eat with you, will I end up in one of those tabloids listed as a mystery boyfriend? I have a girl back home, and I wouldn't want to mess things up with her. Not that I wouldn't want to be your boyfriend," he stammered. "Oh, you know what I mean."

Jan burst out in a gale of laughter. "I'm sorry," she said when she saw the bewildered look on the young man's face. "It's just that I seem to cause problems for someone wherever I go. Don't worry. I'll make sure everyone knows you're my security guard," she promised as she pulled her arm away from his. "I need to stop by the stall before we go to the Cafe, so I can get rid of this silly wig and grab a pen and some pictures for the autograph signing."

Justin was just coming back from his calf sorting event and was elated that he had scored well. "I didn't beat you, of course, Aunt Jan, but I beat Brett. His horse didn't do that well at all. Jim beat him too. I hope you don't mind."

"Mind?" asked Jan. "I'm delighted."

"But, I thought you and he were a thing, aren't you?" he asked.

"No, Justin, we are not a 'thing'; we're just neighbors."

"That's good. Then I won't have to go on pretending that I like him. He's okay, but he's not your type."

"And just what do you think is my type?" asked Jan smiling at her nephew.

"I'm not sure. I'm still working on that, but it's definitely not Brett Kendall."

"Let's change the subject. So, do you think my score is going to stand as a first place finish?" asked Jan.

"No doubt about it. Everyone's talking about it. No one has even come close."

"That's a relief. Now, I've got to get over to the Café to sign some autographs. Want to come? Lots of cute cowgirls over there."

"Sure, it's my turn anyway. Let me grab some of your photos. By the way, you need to have another picture taken. You're much prettier than this one."

"What? You don't like the picture? What's wrong with it?"

"It doesn't show the true you. It's too glamorous. You need to have one taken of you sitting on a fence rail in your hat and boots. That appeals to more cowboys."

"And what makes you think I want to appeal to cowboys?"

"I know you do, you just haven't realized it yet. Come on, let's get going. We only have an hour before our next class, and I'm starved." Turning to Tim Fletcher, he said, "Hey, Tim. If you'd like just to wait here and watch the barn, I can handle the security at the autograph signing. I'll bring you some lunch when we get back."

"Is that all right with you, Miss Taylor?" asked Tim.

Jan smiled at the obvious relief on the young man's face at avoiding the possibility of being pictured with her and a bunch of cowgirls. "She must be special—your girlfriend, I mean."

"She is," Tim answered. "I plan to ask her to marry me at Christmas, but don't say anything to anyone, Justin. I want to surprise her."

"Way to go, man," said Justin slapping Tim on the shoulder. "It's about time. You two have been going together since middle school."

Chapter 14

Jan, Jim, and Justin were waiting for their turn to enter the arena for the Team Penning competition. In this event, a team of three riders must cut three specifically numbered head of cattle from a herd and move them across the starting line to the opposite end of the arena into a fenced pen. The team must complete this whole process within ninety seconds. None of the other cows must cross the starting line except those being penned. Scores for the event are based upon the time and number of cows penned. The event reflects what is required of a working ranch horse.

The three of them agreed that Raven should be the horse to cut the numbered cows from the herd and run them down the wall to Jim, who would keep them at the opposite end of the arena until it was time to drive them into the pen. It was Justin's responsibility to make sure that none of the other cows, called trash cows, crossed the starting or cow-line.

"Let's go get 'em," whispered Justin as they entered the gate.

The flagman gave them the signal to begin the penning and handed them their assigned number for the three cattle they were to pen. Jan headed Raven immediately into the herd and directed him toward one of their assigned cows.

Raven calmly cut the cow from the herd and quickly moved it away from the others. Jim immediately ran the cow to the other end of the arena and held it there. Jan then headed Raven back for the second cow. Justin was kept busy riding back and forth slowly in front of the cow line keeping the herd behind it. Penning requires careful control of the movements of the riders so that the herd doesn't get restless and scatter. The last thing that a penning team wants is a stampede in the arena.

On their second cut, they got lucky—two of their numbered cows were right beside each other in the herd. Raven easily cut out the two cows and separated both of them from the herd at once. Jan quickly ran both cows down the wall to Jim. Justin checked once more to make sure that none of the rest of the herd had crossed the starting line. Satisfied that the herd was contained, he raced to the end of the arena to help with the penning. Working together, the three of them quickly drove the separated cows into the makeshift pen. Glancing around again to verify that the herd was still behind the starting line, Jan raced Raven inside of the pen, threw her hand in the air, and yelled, "Time."

Thirty-four seconds flashed on the large overhead screens hanging from the ceiling in the center of the Jim Norick arena.

"Best time of the day," said the announcer.

"Way to go, everyone," shouted Justin as they rode out of the arena. "Man what luck when Raven cut out both of the last two calves at the same time. We don't typically have that much luck."

"I couldn't believe it," muttered Jim.

"Hey, you two, Raven and I meant to get those two calves at once," Jan argued. "That wasn't luck; it was strategy."

"Yeah, and you just planned that they would be standing next to each other in the herd, right?" teased

Justin.

"No, that was luck, but when I saw them together, I had Raven go for both of them at once. And, Justin, you were right there to close the gap to keep any of the rest of the herd from following the two cows. Good timing and great instincts. We make a good team."

"Yes, we do," said Jim rubbing his shoulder.

"You all right?" asked Jan.

"Yeah, just a little sore."

Jan rode up beside Jim and reached over to touch his forehead. "You're feverish. We need to get you back to the barn and take you to the hospital. All that jostling around back and forth couldn't have felt good."

"I don't feel too great," Jim admitted.

"Good god, Jim. There's blood on the back of your shirt," shouted Justin. He immediately dug his cell phone out of his jeans and dialed 911. He instructed the ambulance to meet them outside the Super Barn. When he saw Jim start to sway back and forth, he quickly jumped off his horse and got on the back of Jim's to hold him in the saddle.

Jan immediately grabbed the reins of the other two horses and headed for the barn at a full gallop. By the time they got there, Jim was unconscious. Justin easily lifted him from the saddle and laid him on the ground just as the ambulance arrived. Thank goodness there are always some emergency vehicles on the grounds during a big event like the World Show.

The EMTs immediately ripped Jim's shirt open and began to provide pressure on the wound to stop the bleeding. Justin grabbed the three horses from

Jan and ran them back into the barn. Jan could hear him yelling for his mom.

"Are his vital signs stable," asked Jan of an EMT monitoring Jim's blood pressure and heart rate.

"His blood pressure is dropping. What's the wound on his shoulder? It looks like a gun shot."

"It is," muttered Jan.

"He may have some internal bleeding," responded the EMT. He glanced up at Jan for the first time. "My god, are you..?"

"Yes," she interrupted, "I'm Jan Taylor, but do you mind staying focused on my friend here? And, no, he's not my boyfriend, and I didn't shoot him in case you plan to talk to reporters."

"We're going to have to transport him to the hospital right away," answered the EMT, appropriately embarrassed. "Are you going to the hospital with him?"

"No, I am," yelled Lacey running out of the barn at breakneck speed with Justin right behind her. "Oh, my god, Jim. Don't you dare die on me," she cried. Jan grabbed her by the shoulders and embraced her until they had Jim loaded on to a stretcher.

"We'll take care of everything here," Jan assured her, "and then we'll come right to the hospital. Call us as soon as you hear anything. Don't worry, he's too tough to die."

"That's what I thought about Robert," sobbed Lacey.

One of the EMTs helped Lacey into the ambulance, and they roared out of the parking lot. Justin put his arm around Jan's waist. "He'll be fine, Aunt Jan. He's as tough as they come," he whispered, but his raspy vcice betrayed his own emotions.

"This is all my fault," responded Jan. "I shouldn't have let him ride, but I knew how good he was, and I wanted the points for Raven. What a heartless, selfish witch I am."

"No, this isn't your fault. It's no one's fault. Jim would have been disappointed if you hadn't let him ride. He might have thought you were still angry with him for going to work for Brett Kendall."

"Please don't utter that man's name in my presence ever again," Jan responded as she stomped off toward the barn. "If there's anyone to blame for this cockamaney mess, it's Brett Kendall. Come on, we've got to get the horses cooled down and find Jamie, so we can get over to the hospital." She suddenly stopped short. "Shoot. What time is it? I'm supposed to pick Roger up at the airport. Never mind, I'll just text him and tel him to grab a cab. You go find Jamie, and I'll take care of the horses. I'll call Beth and let her know what's going on. We need to be at the hospital with your mom in case things don't go well there."

Chapter 15

Lacey paced back and forth in the family waiting lounge of the hospital. The doctor had come out earlier to explain that the stitches in Jim's shoulder had broken loose and that he had lost a lot of blood. He had asked her if by chance she was blood type O positive, the type that Jim needed. She was surprised at something else she and Jim had in common. When she confirmed that her blood type was O positive, the doctor took her immediately to the lab in the hospital where she donated blood for Jim's transfusion. She was now just waiting to hear the results of the surgery and the transfusion.

How strange my life has turned out, she thought. *Not that I'm complaining, but I just didn't expect for Robert to disappear from it. I always thought that we would raise our kids and grow old together on the ranch surrounded by friends and family. I miss him. Now, here I am, worrying about Jim, and praying he doesn't leave me too.*

"Excuse me, Mrs. Livingston," said a young doctor interrupting her thoughts. "I'm Dr. Finn, one of the residents here at the hospital. Mr. Cordrey's doctor sent me out to talk with you."

"How's Jim?" asked Lacey nervously wringing her hands.

"He's doing fine. We've gotten the bleeding under control and are continuing with the transfusion, but we were unable to use the blood you donated."

"Unable to use it? Why?" asked Lacey. "I don't understand. I have donated b ood back home all the time with no problem."

"Would you like to sit down?" asked the obviously nervous young doctor, pointing to a chair near Lacey.

"No, I prefer to stand," said Lacey. "I don't understand what you are trying to tell me."

Dr. Finn shifted uncomfortably on his feet and darted his eyes away from hers. Finally, he cleared his throat and answered, "You're CBC or complete blood count showed an uneven distribution between your white and red blood cells."

"What does that mean in plain English?" asked Lacey collapsing into the nearest chair. "Does it mean I have cancer, or what?"

"Not necessarily," he comforted, reaching out to touch her hand. "It just means that you should visit your doctor and have a complete physical immediately. The sooner we can diagnose the cause of the unequal distribution, the quicker we can restore it to normal."

Lacey reached up and put her hand across her left breast, recalling that she had thought she had felt a lump there a month or so ago.

Dr. Finn looked at her closely. "Do you suspect that you might have breast cancer, Mrs. Livingston?" he asked.

"I, uh, I don't know," muttered Lacey. "A month or so ago, I thought I felt a lump, but it seems to have gone away."

"Why don't you come on back with me to the clinic? I can do a brief examination now, and then you can follow up with your doctor as soon as you return

121

home."

As Lacey stood up to follow the intern, Justin came flying through the door of the waiting room. Lacey quickly looked at Dr. Finn and softly muttered, "Not now. I'll take care of this as soon as I get home." Seeing the concerned look in the young man's eyes, she smiled and reached out to take hold of his hand. "I promise," she said. "I have a lot of reasons to take care of myself," she smiled.

"What's going on, Mom?" asked Justin. "Are you okay? You look pale?" He glanced to the doctor, who looked away.

"Nothing's wrong, Justin," assured Lacey, reaching up and patting her handsome son on the cheek. "The young doctor was just telling me that Jim is doing fine, but he had to have a transfusion because he lost so much blood. The stitches evidently tore loose and caused the bleeding." Turning to Dr. Finn, she asked, "When do you think we can see Jim?"

"I, uh, I'll go and check to see where they are with the transfusion, and then I'll come back out to let you know. I'll be right back."

"Are you sure, you're all right, Mom," prodded Justin. "It looked like you were having a pretty serious conversation when I came into the room."

"I've just been nervous about Jim. He's very important to me, you know," she said.

"I know. He's important to all of us," said Justin. "You know, Mom, dad would never want you to be alone," he said putting his arm around his mother's shoulders.

Lacey leaned against him, "I know, sweetie. I know."

122

"Jim obviously cares about you. He cares about all of us. Jamie and I don't want you to... well," he hesitated, "we don't want you to hold off marrying Jim because you worry about how we'll feel. We want you to have someone to care for you like dad always did. You're still young. Heck, maybe I could still have that little brother I always wanted."

"Justin," said Lacey laughing. "I'm not that young."

"Yes, you are. A lot of women have children in their forties, and you just turned forty this year."

"How in the world did this conversation get turned around to talking about me getting pregnant? Where's Jamie? And Jan?"

"Jamie's pole bending class had a three-way tie for first, so they had to have another go round. Jan stayed to cheer her on. They'll be here as soon as the class is over." Justin reached in his pocket and pulled out a wrapped sandwich and a banana. "Here, I brought you something to eat. I know you haven't eaten all day, so you sit down, and I'll go find a vending machine for a soda."

Lacey watched him dart off down the hall at a jog. *He is such a compassionate young man, just like his dad.* She sighed and sat down in the nearest chairs. She felt old and tired. She also was scared. *What if I do have cancer? Who would take care of my kids? Jan and Beth both have careers, and it would be unfair to ask them to change their lives. I know they would do anything I asked, but I don't want to have someone else attend Jamie's college graduation, pick out her wedding dress, and hold her first child. I want to do those things. Stop it; stop it,* she scolded. *You're borrowing trouble before you know you have any.* She opened the sandwich and smiled. Justin had added every condiment she liked.

"What a wonderful husband he will be someday," she said aloud.

"Mrs. Livingston?" said the young resident.

Lacey jumped at the sound of another voice in the room.

"I'm sorry. I didn't mean to startle you. You can come in to see Mr. Cordrey now if you'd like."

"Thank you. I'll just wait until my son returns, and then we'll come right back. Is Jim doing all right?"

"He's doing fine, but we will be keeping him here overnight this time to monitor his blood pressure and to ensure there are no signs of infection. He isn't very happy about that, so maybe you can assure him that the horse show will survive without him for a few days."

Lacey laughed. "I bet he *is* giving you a rough way about keeping him. He's pretty set in his ways and pretty much thinks he's invincible."

"He's a rancher, Mom," said Justin returning with a can of soda for her. "We are strong and steadfast; that's our mantra." Justin extended his hand to the intern. "Hi, I'm Justin Livingston."

"Nice to meet you. I'm Dr. Finn, a first-year resident here. I just told your mom that you two could come on back to see Mr. Cordrey as soon as you want."

"Great. We'll be back as soon as my mom finishes that sandwich. She needs to eat the whole thing. She has a bad habit of missing meals."

"Not a good way to treat yourself, Mrs. Livingston," responded Dr. Finn. "You'd better listen to your son. When you're ready, Mr. Cordrey is in room 204. Just ask at the nurse's station if you have any trouble finding him. I'll just let him know you'll be in to see him shortly."

Justin plopped down in the chair next to his mom and popped the tab on his can of soda. "How'd I do with the sandwich?" he asked.

"Perfect. It's delicious, but I don't feel like I can eat it right now," answered Lacey.

"Well, just how bad do you want to see Jim?"

"Justin, you are relent ess." She leaned over and gave him a kiss on the cheek.

"Yes, I am," he said.

Chapter 16

As soon as the airplane landed, Roger turned on his Blackberry. He had two text messages from Jan. He tapped the screen to open the last message. "Hmm," he muttered. "I'm obviously on my own to get to the World Show. Okay, I can handle that," he said flipping his phone off to save what little battery he had left.

He had been worrying the whole trip about how he would react when he saw Beth. *If only I could talk with her*, he thought. *Maybe I could convince her to give me another chance*. He grabbed his carry-on and headed into the airport in search of the taxi stand. As he turned the corner beyond the secured area, he stopped short, letting his bag drop to the floor. *Am I hallucinating or is that actually Beth standing there staring at me with tears in her eyes?* "Beth?" he whispered.

Beth couldn't restrain herself any longer. She stumbled toward him and grabbed him around the neck. "I love you; I love you; I love you," she sobbed falling into his arms.

Roger lifted her in the air and swung her around. "I love you too," he said. "I love you too. Oh, my god. I love you. I am so sorry I hurt you. I'll never cause you a single moment of pain again, I promise. Just don't leave me. Please, don't ever leave me again."

The crowd of passengers smiled as they passed the couple standing in the middle of the aisle, locked in an embrace that seemed impenetrable. "Isn't love grand?" muttered a middle-age woman as she passed by. "What ever happened to us feeling that way?" she asked poking the man with her in the side.

"If you looked like her, I'd be holding you that tight too," snarled the man.

Roger gently lowered Beth to the ground. "Oh, my god, what a wonderful, wonderful surprise. I've dreamed of holding you again every night for the past two years." He buried his face in her hair and let the tears pour from his eyes. "I love you," he whispered again. "Please, please, say you'll marry me. Please," he begged.

"The sooner, the better," answered Beth, smiling up at him. She cupped his face in her hands and tenderly wiped away his tears. "I've been so foolish to keep you away. I'm sorry; so sorry."

Roger reached into his pants pocket and pulled out a small, tattered box. "I've been carrying this around with me everywhere I went for the past two years." He opened the box and took out a large emerald-cut diamond and slipped it on Beth's finger. "I was afraid I was going to have to turn it into a lapel pin."

"It's the ring I threw at you the last time we were together, isn't it?"

"Yes. I still have the scar. See?" he said pointing to the small indentation on his forehead.

"Ooh. Sorry about that," Beth said linking her arm inside of Roger's and holding her hand out to admire the ring. "It still fits, and it still sparkles," she said. "Now all we have to do is get our old fit and sparkle back."

Roger leaned over to softly kiss her lips. "Now, how do we break this to everyone else? Do you think that'll be a problem?"

"Absolutely, not," assured Beth. "Both of my sisters have been nagging me about giving our relationship another chance. They'll be thrilled, and I can finally get a respite from their not so subtle hinting."

"Wow, this was a whole lot easier than I thought it would be," said Roger beaming proudly. "On the airplane, I must have run a thousand scenarios about seeing you here and about how we would act toward one another. I certainly didn't picture this scene."

Beth laughed. "I just couldn't run the risk that you would be too polite or too much of a coward to come to me. So, I hopped a cab to come to you. And, I hope you know that it probably cost me some commissions to close up my booth to come out to meet you. You'd better be worth it."

Roger hugged her once more, and then leaned over to pick up her cane that had fallen on the floor. "I am. I absolutely am," he assured her. "Now, since you took a taxi out here, I assume you know how to find one to take us back to the hotel. And, please, fill me in on what the heck is happening. Jan's texts were cryptic, but she sounded like things were a mess."

On the way back to the hotel, Beth described the events of the past three days. Roger was worried about how all this would be affecting Jan's performance on Friday. He knew that when things weren't right in her personal life, it was hard for her to find the strength she needed for the high-energy shows she performed. "My good god. What a mess. How is Jan holding up with all of this?"

"I hate to tell you, but she's a mess too. She looks absolutely lost. I'm not sure what's going on with her."

Roger gazed out the window of the cab and drew in a deep breath. "I worry about her," he finally said. "She seems to be so torn between her music and the ranch. I don't know how to help her."

"Just let her work it out. Jan's a strong woman; she'll figure it out on her own. All you need to do is to be there for her. That's all any of us can do right now."

Roger pulled Beth close to him. "You are so good for me," he muttered. "I've missed your calming ways and your deep insights."

Beth let her head drop against Roger's shoulder. *This is where I belong,* she thought. *I am finally feeling whole again.*

Chapter 17

Jan slipped the strap of her acoustic guitar over her head and grabbed hold of Raven's mane to swing herself onto his back. Lacey had called and told her not to bother coming out to the hospital. Jim was fine, but they wanted him to get some rest and preferred that they limit his visitors. Roger had texted her saying he would be out to the show grounds in an hour or so with a wonderful surprise for her. *I wonder what he considers a surprise—probably good news about the sales of my new album.*

"Where are you going with your guitar and Raven?" asked Jamie. "I thought you were going over to see if you could find Beth to tell her about Jim."

Jan leaned over to run her fingers through Ravens long mane to straighten it. "I did go over to see her, but she wasn't there. It isn't like her to close her booth early. I hope she's not sick or something. She still doesn't answer her phone."

"She always turns her phone off," replied Jamie. "She only turns it on to make a call. We have to go out to her studio at the ranch all the time if we want her for something."

Jan laughed. "She really is a recluse, through and through. Anyway, I'm just going to ride Raven out in the back fields for a while. Hopefully, we can slip away without a crowd of onlookers. I just want to let the cool evening breeze blow through my head and clear the clutter." Raven pawed at the ground indicating he was ready to get started. Jan reached out and patted his withers. "I've been working on a new song, and it sometimes helps to feel the cadence of Raven's easy lope to get the rhythm and beat of my songs."

"You two are quite a pair," said Jamie. "It's amazing to watch the two of you in action. It's like you just melt together in one continuous mass of fluid motion."

"Raven can read me better than most humans can. He just seems to know how to move to soothe me. I can't describe it. It isn't like I trained him that way. He's just a supersensitive animal; it's like our spirits are entwined somehow." She leaned forward and hugged Raven's strong neck. "Does all this sound crazy?"

"No, it doesn't. I just envy the connection you two have. When you're not at the ranch, he's despondent and lost, and he seems to know when it's time for you to come back. Justin and I have talked about how he just seems to know that you're near. He perks right up and paces around in his stall anticipating your return." Jamie rubbed Raven's muzzle and patted him on the neck. "It's spooky sometimes, but he's never wrong. You're always back within hours of his sudden change in disposition. Isn't that right, fellow?"

Raven tossed his head in the air and let out one of his piercing screams. Jamie covered her ears. "Now that's one habit of his that I wish you would break. He catches me off guard every time with that high pitched blast and just about ruptures my ear drums."

"Sorry about that," apologized Jan. "That's just the call of the wild that's still part of his spirit. OK, we're off. Are you all right here, or do you want to come with us?"

"No, I'm good. Richard is coming by in a few minutes, and we are heading over to the Margarita

131

Party. When you get back, why don't you come and join us. Lots of good two steppin' music."

"Thanks, but I'm going to head back to the hotel right after I meet up with Roger. He should be here in an hour or so. Tomorrow is going to be a tough show and rehearsal day, so I want to go to bed early." She threw her niece a kiss and headed Raven out across the paddock area. She liked to ride him bareback instead of having a stiff saddle separating her from the feel of his strong, muscled back.

~~~~~

Brett waited for her to pass by the exercise pens and then climbed on his horse to follow her. He had volunteered to relieve the Fletcher family from 'Jan duty', so they could enjoy some of the evening festivities.

As he turned his horse away from the fence, he kept enough distance from her so that she wouldn't notice him, while making sure that he would be close enough to protect her if someone else tried to get too close. When she reached the open area beyond the parked trailers, she slowed Raven to a walk. She reached behind her to swing around her guitar that was dangling down her back. Brett watched as she let loose of Raven's mane and urged him into a slow lope.

After a few minutes, Raven slowed to a walk and Brett could hear her clear voice floating toward him on the evening breeze. He couldn't distinguish the words, but he knew he had never heard the song before. It had a haunting melody and sounded a little softer than her typical up-beat songs.

Brett was amazed at how Raven just picked up the beat and moved in time with her singing. He felt like he was watching something spiritual as the two of them moved together to the rhythm of the guitar. *She's so talented and beautiful,* he thought to himself. *She's everything I've been searching for in a woman—strong, independent, and smart. But, she's younger than me, not so much in years but in her place in life. The seven years difference in our age isn't the issue. But she's just starting her career, and I'm finally reaching the point in mine where I'm on a maintenance path. I'm ready to settle down and start a family. She isn't ready for that—not by a long shot.* He sighed and felt a heaviness in his chest that he had never experienced before.

He was used to getting what he wanted. There was always a way to get whatever he set his mind to, but this time—this situation—was not the same. It was much more complicated than any of the hundreds of intricate business deals he had arranged. He could keep his personal wants and desires in check during a business deal, but this one was all about his emotions and desires. *There has to be a way; there has to be,* he decided.

~~~~~

A sudden shift in the direction of the wind caused Raven to pick up the scent of another stallion, and he began to snort and prance. "Easy Raven," said Jan. "What is it?" She glanced around her and finally spotted the lone rider lurking in the shadows just at the edge of the area where she had been riding. "Hmm, fellow," she said rubbing Raven on the side of his neck. "I think we have company."

She headed Raven toward the rider assuming it was one of the Fletchers, who was stuck with guard duty. As she got closer, she instantly recognized Brett Kendall and slowed Raven to a walk. "Brett?" she called out, "Is that you?"

Brett hesitated before answering, trying to decide if he should ride away or stay. "Hey," he called out at last. "I didn't mean to interrupt your ride, but I offered to give the Fletcher's the night off."

Jan immediately felt a pang of disappointment that he was only there to protect her. "I'm fine," she said. "I'm sorry if I've become such a bother to everyone, but I really don't feel any need for protection when I'm out here with Raven. He's all the protection I need."

Brett dropped his head, and Jan realized she had irritated him again with her dismissive comment and talk about Raven. "I didn't mean to suggest that I don't appreciate all that you and the others have done to help me here," she called out. *Why am I always saying the wrong thing to this man*, she admonished.

"I like the melody of the song you were singing," muttered Brett. "It's definitely different from your others."

He obviously intends to keep the conversation impersonal, decided Jan. She drew in a deep breath and audibly sighed. "Yeah, it is," she muttered. "It's something I've had on my mind for the past couple of days. I'm hoping it gives some hope to a little girl I met. Her sister is evidently in the final stages of cancer, and I was trying to think of some way to help my little friend through this. She's supposed to be at the concert Friday night."

"You're such a study in contrasts. One minute you're riding into a herd of cattle and chasing a cow at full speed down the side of a wall; then, in the next minute, you're trying to comfort a complete stranger with a song. Just who are you, Miss Jan Taylor?"

"If only I knew; if only," she said looking up at Brett with a look of desperation in her eyes.

Brett stared at her, and he was sure that she

could see the passion in his eyes, but he didn't care. His throat tightened, and his whole body went rigid with desire. "Jan" he whispered in a voice so full of longing that he could hardly get the words out. "I, I wish I could help you decide what you want from life, but I can't. No one can. You have to decide that. All I know is that I, uh, I…" he stopped and stared deep into her eyes, then suddenly he spun his horse around and rode off at a full gallop.

Jan just watched in amazement as he rode out of sight, and probably out of her life. Tears flowed like rivers from her eyes, and she leaned over to bury her face in Raven's thick mane. 'Oh, Raven," she cried. "Who am I? Who am I?"

Raven turned around and slowly walked back toward the isolated field, letting her rest against his powerful neck. He began to lope slowly around the paddock, rocking her back and forth, as he circled the field in the cool November night.

Chapter 18

Jan was startled when she heard someone calling her name. She sat up suddenly—almost throwing herself off Raven's back. She had obviously fallen asleep resting her head against Raven's neck. Raven instantly stopped moving when he felt her losing her balance, so she could correct herself to avoid falling off. "Who is it?" she called out to the dark figure running toward her.

"Thank goodness," shouted Roger. "I thought you had passed out or something. How could you possibly be comfortable in that crazy position, and what are you doing out here in the middle of nowhere alone? I've been searching for you for over an hour. You shouldn't do this to me. I can't take it."

"What in the heck are you babbling about?" asked Jan. "I'm just trying to get some peace and quiet out here. What time is it, anyway."

"It's after eight."

"Really? I had no idea that I'd been out here for two hours. I must have fallen sound asleep." She reached out to touch Raven's sweaty withers. "I'm so sorry fellow. I didn't mean to work you so long." She slid off his back and on to the ground. "Come on, Roger. I've got to get him back to the barn and dried off. He'll catch pneumonia out here in this cold air."

"What about you?" asked Roger. "Aren't you cold out here in that flimsy jacket? You can't afford to catch a cold now. Here, put this on," he said wrapping her tightly in his leather jacket.

"Quit worrying about me. The heat from Raven's body has kept me warm. It's him that we need to worry about."

As they entered the barn, Justin stepped out of the tack room. "What the heck?" he yelled. "How did he get so hot and sweaty? What in the heck were you doing, Aunt Jan."

"I fell asleep, and he must have just kept moving in circles in a slow lope. Help me get him cooled down—hurry Justin."

Jan knew that Raven was in trouble if they couldn't get him cooled down right away. She grabbed a cooling sheet and threw it over him to keep him from chilling in the crisp night air, and then she led him toward the washing area. She knew there was only one bay that was heated. "Justin run ahead of us, and see if you can get us into the heated bay, so we can wash him down and avoid having him get chilled."

"Jan," said Roger, "don't you want to hear my good news?"

"Oh, for heavens sake, Roger. Not now, not now," she said pushing past him. She reached over and patted Raven's steamy withers, "I'm so sorry, fellow. I'm supposed to be taking care of you, and you always end up taking care of me."

By the time they arrived at the bathing area, Justin had convinced several of those in line to let them go ahead of them with Raven. Jan could see the disgusted looks from the other horse people as she led the steamy Raven into the shower. She knew that they had a right to be angry. There was no excuse for working a horse as long as she had worked Raven.

"Let me get this straight," said Justin spraying tepid water around Raven's feet. "You fell asleep, and Raven loped around for over an hour? How could you have stayed on him if you were asleep?"

"I don't know. I told you that he has this incredible lope that's like sitting on a slow-moving rocking chair. There's no bounce, no jarring, just an even rocking motion." Jan reached up and touched Raven's back. "I think he's getting rid of some of that heat. The tepid water seems to be doing the trick."

"You'd better hope he doesn't get pneumonia," responded Justin. "You women had better start getting your head's on straight. I can't keep up with your mood swings and catastrophes. Y'all are like herding a bunch of cats."

Jan reached over and tapped the back of Justin's hat sending it forward over his eyes.

"Hey," he shouted. "Don't mess with the hat."

"I admit it. I was stupid here. I do have to get my head on straight. I'm just grateful that Raven is in such good shape. He'll be fine. I'm just sorry I let him get so hot on such a cool night."

After an hour of washing, drying, and massaging by Jan and Justin, Raven's temperature returned to normal. He pranced proudly back to his stall alongside of Jan with nostrils flaring and head lifted. It was as if he was trying to show the world that he was tough and proud of it.

When they came around the corner of Raven's stall, Jan stared at amazement at Roger, who was leaning up against the stall with his arm around Beth's waist.

"Surprise," said Roger, pulling Beth closer to him. "I've been trying to tell you about us since I got here."

"Now this is news worth celebrating," said Jan. "Finally, I can take you two off my list of people to worry about. How did this all happen?"

"Spare me the details," moaned Justin. "I'm out of here. Somewhere over there at the Margarita Party there's a cowgirl waiting for me to give her a twirl around the dance floor."

"I think we should all go over and celebrate," said Beth. "I haven't been to one of those parties for years."

"See you over there " said Justin jogging toward the door.

Jan put Raven in his stall and glanced out between the metal bars at Roger and Beth, who seemed lost in their own little world. *Thank goodness*, she thought. *I know this will work this time. It has to. They need each other.*

"What do you say, Sis," asked Beth. "Are you up for a couple of margaritas and some country two-steppin'?"

"You know, I do believe I am," said Jan, smiling at the sparkle in Beth's eyes—a sparkle that Jan hadn't seen for more than two years.

~~~~~

The Margarita Madness Party was in full-swing when they entered the pavilion. Jamie saw them and let out one of her piercing whistles to attract their attention.

"And she complains about Raven's piercing screams," said Jan leaning toward Beth. Jan waved and made her way through the crowd to their table. Richard jumped up to give her his seat and grabbed another chair for Beth.

"What would you ladies like?" asked Richard.

"I don't want anything but a nice, big glass of

139

water," said Jan.

"You're not getting a sore throat are you? " asked Roger.

"No, Roger. Quit worrying. I'm just thirsty; that's all." Jan sighed. *I have to tell him to stop hovering,* she thought. *He's like an old mother hen trying to keep all of his baby chicks in a row.*

"What about you, honey," he said turning to Beth. "Regular, on the rocks, no salt?"

"You remembered," said Beth, smiling up at him.

"Of course, I remembered. I remember everything about you."

"Thank god, Justin's not here," said Jamie giggling. "He'd be gagging right about now."

"Hey, young'un," snapped Beth. "Let me enjoy this. Believe me; I know it won't last forever."

Jan glanced around the room looking for Brett, but she didn't see him among the cowboys packed into the room. *I have to quit thinking about that man,* she scolded herself. *He has ridden away twice and not looked back. Anyway, the timing is not right for us right now.* She sighed and took a big gulp of water, which immediately went down the wrong way. She coughed until she thought she would choke to death. Finally, Jamie slapped her across the back, and the coughing started to subside.

"Oh no, that's not good for the vocal cords," moaned Roger. "Why don't we take you back to the hotel?" he offered. "You've had enough of this cool night air, and you need to get some warm food in you."

Jan slid off the stool, but just as she was about

to leave, the announcer called out her name on the loud speaker. "Hey guys and gals, look who's trying to sneak out of here without a song—Miss Jan Taylor. I bet if we coax her with a big ol' Oklahoma round of applause, we can get her to sing one of her new songs as a preview for her Friday night concert. How about it, Miss Taylor?"

Jan held her hand up to shield her eyes as a spotlight shone on her. She glanced toward Roger, who simply nodded his assent. She knew there was no escape, so she headed toward the stage. The band had already started to play one of her favorites, and immediately she felt revived. She loved this kind of intimate setting—a room full of cow folk out on the town to have a good time. From the small stage, she could see friends that she recognized. Their presence momentarily carried her back to Texas, and she was full of energy and pleasurable feelings. *This is what I love. These are the people my songs are about. They understand the feelings in my songs because they have lived my life*, she thought. As she sang, she looked out at the crowd clapping and singing along with her. She was amazed at how many of them knew every word of the song. She guessed it was probably like that at her big concerts, but the blinding lights and the distance between her and the audience made it difficult for her to see the pleasure that the fans felt for her music. She sang one more song then apologized for having to leave by saying, "Hey, folks, this cowgirl has a heavy show schedule tomorrow, and she needs to get some rest. Love y'all," she said, "you're my kind of folks."

Roger and Richard appeared at her side and ushered her through the crowd and out into the brisk November night. "Now that was fun," she said turning to Roger.

Roger smiled. "Yeah, you looked like you were having a good time up there tonight, but life's not all about fun, Jan. Sometimes it's about work and sacrifice. Road tours may seem like work, but they are part of the sacrifice you have to make to get to the top—assuming, that is, that you want to get to the top."

Jan stopped and looked up at him. "Honestly, Roger, I don't know what I want. The closer I get 'to the top'—whatever that means—the farther away I seem to be getting from who I am and from why I started out singing in the first place."

Roger reached out and pulled her close. "Life is about trade-offs, Jan. I want to help you, but you have to tell me what you want."

Jan leaned against him. "I know, Roger. You've been wonderful. All I know is that I love music. I truly believe that music reaches the soul faster and deeper than any other means of communicating. I love writing songs about life, and I love singing them to people who understand their message."

"That's why I like your music, Miss Taylor," said Richard. "There's a message in every song, and depending on my mood, I can find one of your songs that will either lift me up or just let me feel the moment."

"See," said Roger. "There you go. You do reach people—lots of people—people you would never be able to reach without getting out there and singing to them. I know you can't see them when you sing in a big arena, but it doesn't mean that they don't hear you. And, trust me, not many people would spend money on a CD of someone they never heard of before." He reached down and lifted her chin, so he could see into her eyes. "Your songs make a difference, Jan, but it's all about trade-offs."

"I know; I know. I'm just not sure how much I want to trade away." She raised up on her tiptoes and

142

kissed Roger on the cheek. "You're a great agent, Roger, and I'm sure you're going to be an even greater brother-in-law. I'm really happy for Beth and for you."

"Me too," said Roger. "Now let's go, so you can get your beauty rest—in bed, not on Raven's back. I'll drive you back." Then, turning to Richard, he said, "Let Beth know that I will be back in a shake," he said.

"I can get back on my own," protested Jan.

"Trade-offs, Jan. One of the things you need to trade away is the right to run around, unprotected at night by yourself. Anyway, I want to hear about this Brett Kendall character. Beth tells me that he makes you smile."

"Hmm, he did make me smile," Jan admitted. "But there's not much else to tell. My cowboy rode away."

"I seriously doubt that," replied Roger. "More than likely, he had the door slammed in his face." Roger opened the door to the truck and helped Jan get in. "You've got to learn how to let others into your private, little life, Jan. Otherwise, you're going to end up as a miserable, worn-out cowgirl riding on a broken-down, old horse—not a pretty picture is it?"

Jan just stared at him in amazement. Finally, she muttered, "No. That's not a very pretty picture."

Chapter 19

Lacey sat down in one of the straight-backed chairs next to Jim's hospital bed. She watched him as he seemed to be sleeping peacefully. Her mind drifted back in time to when they were young. As teenagers, she, Jim, and Robert were inseparable. Jim lived in town with his mother who owned a small diner, but as soon as he was old enough, he went to work on their ranch for her dad. His mom died of lung cancer during his senior year in high school, and Jim moved out to the ranch, staying in the bunkhouse with the other ranch hands. Robert's father owned a small ranch that adjoined theirs, but Robert spent his free time with her and Jim.

Every Friday night, the three of them loaded their horses in a trailer and headed out to the local rodeo grounds. Her mom and dad would bring Jan and Beth to watch them compete and to let Jan enter in the junior rodeo. Lacey smiled as she remembered how everyone marveled at how that little red-headed girl would fly around the barrels, making the turns so sharp and fast that her pony was practically laying on its side. Jan would bring home a trophy every weekend in sheep riding and youth barrel racing. The rodeo managers also asked her to sing the *Star Spangled Banner* every night she was there. In fact, it was at the rodeo, when she was just six years old, that Jan first sang in public.

Every weekend, all year long was a rodeo weekend. Jim and Robert rode bulls and were partners in calf roping. She competed in the senior division barrel racing until Jan got old enough to compete against her and consistently beat her. Jim was the bull-riding champion at the local rodeos around the state, but he could never afford to compete at a national level. The time and expense of traveling just wasn't possible for him.

When they were young, she and Jim were together all the time. Later, when she was just turning nineteen, she realized that their feeling for one another was more than mere friendship. She could tell by the way he looked at her that he cared for her in a way other than as just a friend. He had started to tell her one night how he felt, but they were interrupted by Robert's sudden appearance in the barn. That same night, Robert proposed to her. She remembered hoping that Jim would ask her too, but she knew that he would never propose to her once Robert had. He was too loyal of a friend to compete with him for her hand.

The night before her wedding, she and Jim were alone in the barn, and she had asked him if he knew of any reason why she shou dn't marry Robert. He looked at her for a long time and reached out to pull her close to him. He hugged her tightly and then suddenly pulled away. He looked at her with eyes brimming with tears, and had simply replied, *'No, I can't think of anyone more deserving of you than Robert.'* He then turned and walked out of the barn slamming the door as he left.

Now, she sat in silence remembering the disappointment that she had felt more than twenty years ago. It wasn't that she didn't love Robert, because she did. It was just that she had loved Jim more.

Jim began to stir, and she reached out and gently patted his hand. "How are you feeling?" she asked softly.

145

"Like a caged animal," he said. "Why won't they let me out of here? I really feel fine," he replied, smiling his broad, handsome grin.

Lacey stared at him for a moment, and a strange feeling stirred in the pit of her stomach. It had been years since the two of them had actually been alone together. As she looked into his soft, kind eyes, she could feel the tears welling up in her own, and she quickly got up and walked over to the window. "It's going to be a pretty sunset," she muttered softly. "I like sunsets."

"You have always liked the sunsets," said Jim sitting up and swinging his feet over the edge of the bed.

"What are you doing, Jim Cordrey? You stay put in that bed," she said turning around and rushing over to him.

Jim reached out and grabbed her hand. "Stop fussing over me, and marry me," he blurted out. "I know this isn't the most romantic place for a proposal, but it's just that I can't wait any longer. I love you, Lacey; you know I do."

Lacey stared at him in stunned silence.

"The only thing I could think about in my semi-conscious state while they were stitching my shoulder and shoving blood through my veins, was you and the fact that I have never made love to you the way I have dreamed of for so long."

"Jim," she sputtered, "I don't know what to say."

"A simple *yes* would do the trick," he said taking hold of her hand. "I know I don't look like much of a prize with my bare feet dangling from this hideous night gown and without my hat on, but I wasted an opportunity a long time ago to propose to

146

you, and I didn't want to miss another chance. We don't have too many opportunities to be alone, so I'm not going to waste this one. Will you marry me?"

Lacey dropped into the chair and buried her face in the sheet across his lap. "Of course, I'll marry you. I would have married you years ago, if you'd just asked," she sobbed.

Jim reached down and gently raised her head. "I love you," he said kissing her gently on the lips and brushing the tears from her cheeks. "I'm a little late in telling you, but I truly, truly love you," he said pulling her close.

Chapter 20

It was a little after five in the morning when Jamie tapped at the door of Jan's hotel room. Jan immediately opened the door. She was already dressed and frantically searching for the keys to the truck. "I can't find the dumb keys to the truck," she moaned as she headed back to the bed where she had dumped the contents of her purse.

"Maybe because you don't have them," said Jamie dangling the keys in the air. "Don't you remember? Roger drove you home and then came back to the party. He gave me the keys after we all came back to the hotel last night."

"Oh, for heaven's sake. Of course, now I remember. I swear my head is somewhere else all the time any more. I don't know what has gotten into me." She scraped together the things scattered on the bed and dumped them back into her purse.

"Love plays funny tricks with your mind," taunted Jamie.

"Well then, that certainly can't be the reason for my absentmindedness," snapped Jan whirling around and bumping Jamie with her hip as she walked past her, "because I am definitely not in love." She opened the door and made a sweeping bow, "You first, my dear," she said smirking at Jamie.

Jamie tossed her head back and laughed. "Yeah, right," she mocked. "Come on, my dear Aunt Scatterbrain, you had better clear your mind. You have to remember the reining pattern today, you know."

"Don't you worry your pretty, little head. Raven and I have the reining contest in the bag. I have to admit, though, I'm not so sure about the pleasure class. He still doesn't like it if anyone crowds him into the rail."

"And they probably will crowd you," warned Jamie. "Some of these trainers are ruthless out here. The stakes connected to the pleasure class are high. The money for first is considerable, and the recognition is even more important."

"I know." Jan sighed. "Raven and I are bound to be the target since we are the present world champs. This should be an interesting day."

"I don't think the word *interesting* accurately describes it. I think maybe *challenging*, *exasperating*, and *tricky* are better indicators of what you are about to experience."

"Well, aren't you a little ray of sunshine," said Jan. "Do you know something that I don't know?"

Jamie pushed the button for the elevator and turned around to stare at her aunt. "Well, for starters, the King Ranch has a major stake in winning the pleasure class, so they'll be in the ring to make sure you don't win. Secondly, you'll be showing against Brett Kendall, and only you know how that might unglue you."

Jan walked into the elevator and leaned back against the wall. "I've already shown against Brett here, and I've won, so I don't see how that will be an issue. As for the King Ranch, I beat them last year if you recall."

When the elevator reached the garage level, Jamie stepped out of it and placed her hand in front

149

of the door to let Jan exit. "You've never been in the same ring with Brett at the same time," she said. "I think that will make a difference."

Jan followed Jamie through the glass doors to the parking garage. Her mind mulled over what her niece had just pointed out to her. *It was true—she hadn't been in the same arena at the same time with Brett. Will that actually bother me,* she wondered. "I don't think it will make any difference to Raven and me who's in the arena with us. We'll just do our thing and ignore the others. It's what we've always done," she proclaimed.

"Well, you're going to have to prove that to me," said Jamie. She turned around and looked at Jan. "See, it's already bothering you; I can see it in your eyes."

"Shush, Jamie. Let's talk about something else. I've got this under control."

Jamie laughed. "Sure you do."

Justin was already in the barn when they arrived. "Where have y'all been? You're late. You do realize that today is the big one, don't you?"

"We're not any later today than any other day. You're just early and obviously uptight about your own competitions," taunted Jamie.

"Yeah, whatever," responded Justin tossing her Raven's brush.

The morning was as hectic as everyone predicted it would be. Raven was more rambunctious than usual, and Jan had some difficulty getting him to perform the reining pattern during their practice session. Lacey was still at the hospital with Jim, so there was no one to keep the three of them organized and calm. They were scrambling to sort out their numbers and to make sure they internalized the time schedule that Lacey had printed out for them to follow.

"Mom will be here any minute, I know she will," said Jamie.

"How's she going to get here? We have both trucks here," reminded Justin

"Oh, my gosh, you're right. Aunt Jan, can you get hold of Roger and tell him to go and get mom?"

Jan reached for her cell phone and dialed Roger's number. Beth answered in a half-awake state. "What time is it?" she groaned into the phone. "You know I never get up before nine."

"Look, Beth, this is an emergency. You've got to wake up Roger and tell him to go and pick up Lacey at the hospital. We need her here to keep us all on track."

"For heaven's sake, Jan. You're an adult. Can't you do anything for yourself without an entourage of people keeping you together?"

"Beth!" shouted Jan. "Don't mess with me this morning. Get Roger up and send him to pick up Lacey." Jan snapped her phone shut and tossed it into her hat box.

"That sounded like it went well," said Jamie.

"How can people sleep until nine every day? Half of the day is over by then," said Jan, helping to pin Justin's number on the back of his shirt.

Jamie grabbed her cell phone to call her mom, but when she dialed the number, a phone rang in the tack stall, and the three riders looked around to stare at the cell phone lying on the table. "Oh great," said Jamie. "Mom doesn't have her cell phone with her."

"Hey, y'all," greeted Lacey. "You guys missing

151

me, yet?"

"Thank, goodness," said Justin turning around and embracing his mom. "These two are driving me nuts. How'd you get here?"

"Jamie's friend Richard came out to the hospital this morning to check on Jim. He brought me back," said Lacey reaching up to straighten Justin's number on the back of his shirt.

"I'm beginning to believe this guy's a real saint," said Justin. "You'd better hang on to this one, Sis."

"I intend to," replied Jamie beaming from ear to ear.

"How's Jim?" asked Jan.

"He's doing fine. They're going to release him sometime this morning, and I will need to go and pick him up. So give me the keys to one of the trucks," she said holding her hand out.

"You can't leave," said Justin. "Send someone else to pick him up. It's chaos here without you."

"I want to go get him," insisted Lacey. "You guys can handle me being gone long enough to get him."

Jan looked closely at Lacey. She noticed a twinkle in her eyes that she hadn't seen for a long time. She looked serene and happy. Jan smiled. "We'll be just fine. You do what you need to do for Jim. It's about time you put him first in your life."

Justin and Jamie stared at their mom's beaming face and exchanged a knowing smile with each other. "Yeah, Mom. Once you get us started, we'll be okay," said Jamie reaching out and giving her mom a quick hug.

152

Lacey smiled at the three of them and grabbed the schedule from the wall "Okay, let's see who needs to be where this morning," she said. "Jan, you're up first. Let's get Raven ready."

~~~~~

Jan arrived early for the reining class and was waiting in the holding area for her run. For some reason, she was nervous, a feeling she had never experienced before in this particular event. *What's wrong with me,* she wondered. I *have to get a grip on myself. Raven is bound to feel my tension.* She hopped down from the saddle and shook her arms and legs. She rolled her head from side to side and drew in a deep breath.

Raven turned his head to look at her and nickered softly. "I know big fellow, this isn't like me, is it?" moaned Jan.

"Don't tell me the great Jan Taylor is nervous?" said Brett walking his horse up beside Jan. "You look scared. Are you okay?"

"You know, I think my nerves have something to do with you," she blurted out. "You keep riding in and out of my life. I just wish you would stay away and let me do what I know I can do."

Brett tipped his hat and smiled. "I'm flattered to think that I might be the cause of your nervousness, but this past couple of days I've learned that you and Raven are a team—a third person only gets in your way. Neither of you wants or needs anyone else to complicate your exclusive little world." He paused for a moment staring deeply into Jan's eyes.

Jan tried to think of something to say. She just stood there staring into his eyes and wanting him to pull her close and to hold her, but he didn't.

"Have a good ride," he said walking away.

"See. There you go again; you interrupt my life and then walk away. Please, please, stay away from me," she screamed. She grabbed hold of the saddle horn and swung herself into the saddle. The nervousness was gone; it was replaced by a fury that inspired a resolve to show him that he was right—she didn't need him. She had Raven and her music. She didn't have room for Brett or anyone else in her life—not now at least.

The steward called her number, and she entered the arena. She watched as the horse and rider before her finished an impressive ride. "We can do it better," she whispered in Raven's ear. "Let's show them what we can do."

Raven pawed the ground with his front foot, and Jan knew he was ready. Now it was up to her to concentrate on the pattern and to give him the ride of his life. She shook her head and wriggled around in the saddle to get herself focused; then she cued Raven and they walked into the center of the arena and made the turn to face the judges. She let Raven stand quietly for a few seconds. *Here we go*, she muttered to herself as she cued him for the first element.

As they began working the pattern, Jan felt everything slip out of her mind as she simply melted into the saddle, moving in perfect rhythm with Raven. She automatically cued him for each element of the pattern, and he immediately responded with grace and confidence. His final slide was like sitting atop of a fast moving bobsled careening down an ice-covered hill. When they finished, the crowd went wild—whistling, clapping, and stomping their boots on the concrete floor. Jan tipped her hat to the crowd, and reached over to pat Raven on the neck. "We did it, fellow. We did it," she shouted excitedly.

From his position along the rail, Brett marveled at the perfection of horse and rider as Jan and Raven completed a flawless ride. Everyone watching believed that they had just seen a perfect ride—perhaps the first perfect ride ever at this level of competition. When the scorekeeper announced Jan's scores, the crowd and every rider waiting to compete spontaneously booed as the total was just one point off perfect. The booing, hissing, and feet stomping continued for at least five minutes before subsiding and allowing the competition to continue.

Justin rode up beside her as Jan exited the ring. "You were amazing. You've never ridden better in your life. It was a thing of beauty to watch you on the monitor out here. Everyone around me just stared in awe. We knew we were truly watching perfection."

Jan reached over and patted Justin on the shoulder. "Thanks, Buddy. But, evidently at least two of the judges didn't see it that way. Anyway, I'm proud of Raven. He's just an amazing, amazing animal."

"Well, for sure, no one is going to touch that score, so you won't have to worry about another go around for first. Now, you can concentrate on your pleasure class. Did you see now many entries are in the Open Division?"

"Yeah, I did," answered Jan. "Some really good horses and riders are going to be hard to beat. I don't need to win that one, though. I just need to place in the top ten to get the All Around for Raven. His other firsts haven't been matched. If this one holds, then we should be able to win the All Around, don't you think?"

"Yeah, I think his overall points are going to be hard to beat, but you'd better check with mom. She has all of the stats. Still, if I were you, I'd go into the pleasure class with the intention to win. The first-place money could help pay the expenses for the show."

"Right," said Jan. "Money—I always seem to forget about that," she called over her shoulder as she headed Raven back to the barn. "Good luck on your run, Justin."

Chapter 21

When she got back to the stall, no one was there. Lacey had left a note saying that she had gone to pick up Jim at the hospital and that she would be back before the afternoon classes. Jan was pleased that Lacey was finally showing some attention to Jim. Jan liked him and knew that he had loved Lacey from afar since they were young kids. *Everyone's life seems to be in order except for my own,* she thought. *I need to decide what I want and stop the stupid back and forth decision-making. The problem is, I want both—singing and ranching. I also want to have a family; I definitely don't want to end up the way Roger painted my future last night. I just need to figure out a way to have it all. I don't mean to be a greedy witch. I just want to sing and live my life on the ranch surrounded by family. That's surely not too much to ask; lots of performers lead double lives, and they do it well—without hurtful, extra-marital affairs, drugs, and alcohol. I can do this,* she decided, grabbing her guitar and plopping down on a bundle of hay.

She began to sing her new song, keeping her voice low so as not to attract attention. She liked the lyrics of the song but continued to struggle with the melody. She wanted it to have a country beat, and at the same time to create a reverent mood of promise and hope. She also wanted the audience to be able to follow the melody easily and wanted the words to be memorable. Most of all, she wanted the song to touch Melanie and to help her accept her sister's fate without fear and despair.

Roger paused outside of the tack stall listening to the soft sound of Jan's crystal clear voice. When she stopped playing, he leaned his head around the corner of the open stall door, "That's truly beautiful, Jan. I've never heard you sing that song before."

Jan whipped around at the sound of his voice, obviously startled by his sudden appearance. "You scared me," she said. "I didn't think anyone could hear me." She looked closely at Roger. "Did you hear the whole song? What do you think?"

"It's beautiful, Jan. It's certainly different from anything else you've written, but it's the real you—sweet, sincere, and memorable."

"I'm still struggling with the melody a little. Do you think you can get the band to work on it this afternoon before rehearsal tonight? I want to add it to the show tomorrow night. I wrote it for that little girl we met in Arkansas. She's coming to the show with her seven cousins. Her oldest cousin works at the hotel. It's a small world, isn't it? When he told me that she was visiting with them for the holidays, I was thrilled to have the chance to see her again."

"Give me what you've scribbled on that piece of paper," said Roger. "I'll give it to the band this afternoon and let them have a go at it. I think I understand the mood you're hoping for."

"Do you think it's too far off from what the audience is used to hearing from me?"

"It's completely different from your other songs, but I like it. Anyway, this is for your little friend, and I think the words will resonate with her. That's what you want, right?"

"It is," Jan answered. "I just want to share my faith with her. I just hope it gives her the strength that I think she and her family are going to need. I really can't begin to imagine the pain they're feeling right now."

158

Roger reached down to brush away the single tear creeping down the side of Jan's cheek and tilted her face up toward him, "You've got such a sentimental heart," he said. "But you've got plenty of spunk too. It takes both of those things to make it in the crazy world of country music. You can't walk away from it, Jan. You represent what country music is all about—heart and soul."

"I know, Roger. I love working on new songs and sharing them with my fans. It's just the traveling that's wearing on me."

"After the tour, you'll be home between concerts. You'll only have to be gone one weekend a month. The rest of the month I'll have the band come to you. We can build a recording studio right on the ranch."

"That takes money," responded Jan. "It sounds perfect, but it takes lots and lots of money to arrange such things, and I don't have that kind of money."

"Leave the fund-raising to me," said Roger leaning over and kissing her on the forehead. "I've got a lead on an incredibly rich potential sponsor that I think will put up the money for a share of the profits."

"Really? Who?" asked Jan. "Who do you know that is willing to invest that much money in me?"

"Like I said, leave the fund-raising to me. I can't tell you who it is right now. Anyway, why do you care who it is so long as it solves your desire to have the best of two worlds?"

"I can't believe it. Are you sure you can pull this off?"

"Pretty sure; not positive, but I'm fairly confident that I can put this together by Christmas. That would make a nice Christmas gift, don't you agree?"

"Oh my god, it would be the best Christmas gift ever!"

"Now," said Roger "I need directions to the hospital and keys to a truck. I understand that I'm supposed to pick up Jim. Beth and I had to bum a ride out here with one of the Fletchers since we didn't have any transportation of our own. I intend to rent a car as soon as I get back from picking up Jim."

"Oh, my gosh. I'm so sorry. Lacey went to get him. In all the flurry of getting to my reining class, I forgot to call Beth back."

"For Pete's sake, don't tell Beth. She's been moaning and groaning all morning about getting up before nine. She is definitely not a morning person."

Jan laughed. "Neither are you. You two are well-matched. I'm so glad you're back together. Life just seems better when you two are connected. Now, if I can just get Lacey and Jim married off, my life will be just the way it should be."

"Hmm," said Roger frowning at her. "What about you, Jan? Do you intend to be unattached forever? That would be a tragic waste."

"No, I just haven't met the man of my dreams yet, but I will. Somewhere out there is a cowboy who can put up with a wife who darts in and out of town, and who has a split personality. I'm just not ready yet, but it's getting close. I can feel it." She smiled and jumped up from the bale of hay, brushing off the seat of her pants. "Let me walk you over to Beth's booth. I can't wait for you to see her new paintings. Pay special attention to the cowboys in the background of the big painting."

"Why?" asked Roger.

"You'll see. Let's go, so I can get back here to work Raven before this afternoon's class. It's going

160

to be a tough one."

"You can do it. I have faith in you and that crazy horse."

"Thanks. I would like to win this one for Lacey. The money will help pay for some of the expenses that being here has cost her and the ranch. Money, money, money—I hate it," she pouted.

"You also spend it," reminded Roger. "Like that jacket you have on. That had to cost a bundle; and that belt buckle—it couldn't have been cheap."

"Hey, I won that buckle last year—so there. The jacket—well that's a different matter. It's an indulgence." Jan looked at her reflection in the full-length mirror that Jamie had mounted in the stall. The black sequined short jacket with the cascade of glittering crystals streaking across the front and back like the tail of a comet had been expensive, but it was much more modest than many of the jackets worn by other female competitors. "I like this jacket," she defended, "and besides, it can be worn on stage or in the show ring, so actually, it's a bargain."

Roger laughed. "Hey, I'm not saying that you shouldn't have nice things. You should. But, I was just reminding you that luxuries cost money, so the next time you start lamenting about having to worry about money, think about this beautiful jacket and stay focused in reality."

Jan was sitting on Raven in the make-up arena waiting for her section of the Western Pleasure class to start. The class was so big that they had split it into three divisions. She was glad that Brett wasn't visible among the group of riders in her section. This class and the final go-round, assuming that they would make it through the initial cuts, would be her last chances to ride Raven in the show ring while she was here.

When she completed this afternoon's rides, the rehearsals and the Friday night performance would occupy all her remaining time at the World Show. Immediately after the show, she'd have to climb aboard her motor coach to head for Albuquerque, then Phoenix, and finally Dallas before heading home for Thanksgiving and Christmas. She couldn't wait for the holidays and the chance to get back into the swing of daily chores at the ranch.

There was something physically and psychologically healing about walking into the barns at the ranch and knowing exactly what had to be done and how to do it. The work was excellent physical exercise and working with some of the temperamental show horses and studs, like Raven, kept her mentally sharp. Each time she returned from a road trip, as she turned into the lane that led to the ranch, she could feel the cares and woes of everything else in her world just slip away. She thoroughly loved going home.

"Are you and Raven ready for this," asked Justin riding up beside her.

Startled by the interruption of her daydreaming, Jan almost fell out of the saddle, causing Raven to jump around. "Whoa, Raven," she said gently tugging on his reins. "Justin, you startled

162

me."

"You'd better get your head on straight for this class," he warned. "Do you see the guy over there with the big sorrel?"

"Yeah," answered Jan. "I recognize him from some of the earlier shows this year."

"Keep an eye on him. He goes in right after you do, and I overheard him telling some of the other riders that he intended to have his horse's nose right in Raven's tail to upset him."

"Thanks for the warning. I'll do what I can to keep a safe distance from him. Any more last minute advice?"

"Just stay awake, for heaven's sake. Don't take anything for granted in the ring. Everyone will be out to get you this year."

"Why does that have to be?" muttered Jan. "I don't mind the competition, but I resent unfair tactics intentionally plotted to disrupt my ride."

"Just be aware in there," warned Justin again. "Raven can easily win this if you just keep him focused."

"Like I can control his mind—he's going to instinctively respond to an aggressive act. You know as well as I do, I can't expect him not to follow his instincts."

"I would say that's true of most horses, but Raven seems to be the exception when you're around. Anyway, have a good ride. That's all we can ask," called Justin as he turned his horse and headed out of the make-up arena.

After Justin left, Jan rode over to the rider on the big sorrel horse. She wanted Raven to get a chance to get to know the other horse before the class. "Hello there," she called to the rider. She stopped nose to nose with the sorrel so that Raven could see and smell him. "I understand that you follow me into the arena. I just wanted to warn you that if you get too close to Raven, I can't be responsible for what he might do. Instead of burying your horse's nose in his tail, I would suggest that, if you value your horse at all, you might want to keep a clear distance. And, if you intentionally mess with my ride, I can guarantee you that neither you nor anyone connected with you will ever show in an AQHA event again. AQHA definitely takes to task those who engage in any unfair practice." She smiled and tipped her hat at the obviously flabbergasted rider. "Have a nice ride," she said as she swung Raven around and rode off.

When they finally called her section into the arena, she laughed to herself when her would-be-spoiler waited before entering to allow plenty of space between the two horses. Now all she had to do was concentrate on keeping a loose rein and letting Raven show how easily and willingly he responds to subtle cues.

In the pleasure class, judges score the horses on their willingness and responsiveness in transitioning between three gaits—the walk, the jog, and the lope. As the horses move around the arena in both directions, judges are looking for a horse that moves effortlessly and easily and is able to cover a reasonable amount of ground with little effort in a balanced, flowing motion while maintaining the proper cadence for each gait.

The walk is a four-beat gait; the jog is a two-beat gait; and the lope is a three-beat gait. The judges watch carefully, scoring faults if a horse fails to maintain the appropriate cadence throughout the required gait. In addition, the horse must carry its head and neck in a relaxed, natural position, aligning the poll or top of its head slightly above or level with its withers. The rider must maintain a light or loose rein with little or light contact with the horse. The whole point of the pleasure class is to identify horses that truly are a pleasure to ride because they willingly and effortlessly move between gaits at the slightest cue from the rider.

Riders are also required to back their horses. The horse must willingly respond to the cue to back and unhesitatingly back in a straight line without resisting, tossing its head, or excessively swishing its tail.

Jan had no doubt that Raven had given her a perfectly pleasurable ride, so it was no surprise to her or to those watching the class when Raven scored four firsts and one second. The rider on the red sorrel scored four seconds and one first. As they were leaving the arena, he rode up beside her. "I guess we're pretty evenly matched." he said.

"Hmm," responded Jan, "I'm not sure how you figure that." She smiled and rode off, noticing that Brett was in the make-up arena about to enter the last division of the pleasure class groupings. He didn't look her way, and she simply rode out of the arena to await the final go-round.

She positioned Raven so that she could see the video monitor outside of the arena. She watched Brett and his towering, gray stallion as they moved around the arena. *He's getting an excellent ride*, she thought. *He'll obviously be in the go-round. So what—I can handle that, and Raven won't even notice. This is all about Raven, not me,* she reminded herself, wiping her cold, clammy hands on the black jeans she wore under her chaps.

When they announced the placements for the third division, Brett's horse was placed first by three of the five judges and second by two of the others. Of course, each horse would begin with zero points in the final go-round, so earlier placements would not be a consideration in the final placing of the class. She leaned forward and hugged Raven around the neck. "Buddy, you're going to have to carry me this time," she whispered in his ear. "I admit it. Brett's presence in the arena is going to affect me, darn it." Raven nickered softly and tossed his head up and down as if he understood. "You're one amazing animal, my dear friend," she said patting him on the neck and once again wiping her clammy hands on her jeans.

"It looks like we have some serious competition with that Gray horse," said the rider of the red sorrel, riding up beside her again. "Do you know that guy riding him?" he asked, but before she could respond, he continued. "I hear he's some business tycoon. Why in the heck would someone like him be messing around in the horse industry? I've heard that there's also some famous country-western singer who's here competing. I can't believe that people like the two of them would mess around with horses?"

Jan laughed. "Maybe they just like horses." She whirled Raven around and left the confused rider to go and check the working order for the final go-round. As she scanned the list, she was relieved to see that she would be entering the arena second and that neither the red sorrel nor Brett's gray were near her.

When they finally called the horses to begin entering the arena for the final-go-round, she tried to keep her eyes focused on the horse immediately in front of her and intentionally didn't look around for Brett. She forced herself to relax, realizing that Raven would feel her tension. However, for some reason she couldn't explain, she sensed the moment Brett entered the ring, and her eyes were immediately drawn in his direction. As fate would have it, he was directly across the arena from her, always within her peripheral vision. *Oh great*, she thought. *The only horse I can see in his.* She shifted her weight in the saddle and tried to concentrate on Raven's rhythm. From the audience, someone suddenly yelled, "Focus!" She immediately recognized Justin's deep, baritone voice and smiled. He was right; she had to focus on Raven, not on herself, and definitely not on Brett.

The class seemed to go on forever before the steward finally called the riders to the center of the arena for the final backing requirement. Raven backed perfectly, but Brett's horse hesitated slightly, and Jan knew that at this level of competition that would eliminate him from a top placement. She suddenly felt her own excitement of the possibility of winning the final go-round slip away and was surprised at how sad and disappointed she felt for Brett. She was so lost in her concerns for Brett that the steward had to call her number several times to start the lineup for the first-place position according to the scorecard of the first judge.

She remained in first place for each of the remaining scorecards of the various judges. Brett placed consistently in the top nine but never as first or second. The sorrel placed twice as second and three times as third. There was no doubt that Raven had won enough points to secure his All Around award. She and Raven had accomplished what they needed to achieve for the ranch. *Then, why do I feel so sad and disappointed*, she wondered as she took the victory lap around the arena.

"You did it," shouted Justin as he met Jan at the exit gate of the arena. "I thought you were going to lose it there for a while, but you finally pulled it together."

Jan slid down from the saddle, just as Brett rode up beside them.

"Congratulations, Jan," he said. "Raven is truly an amazing horse, and the two of you complement each other perfectly. I don't suppose you would have time to celebrate your win over dinner, would you?"

Jan stared at him unable to utter a sound. Finally, Justin punched her in the side, and she blurted out, "I have rehearsals this evening."

"Right, I forgot," replied Brett as he turned his horse and rode off before she had a chance to say anything else.

"What in the heck is wrong with you?" asked Justin. "Are you going to rehearse all night, for heaven's sake?"

"No, of course not, he just took me by surprise. I just can't think straight when he appears out of the blue like that."

"That's certainly obvious. Look, Aunt Jan, you evidently are interested in the guy. Why don't you call him and make arrangements for a midnight dinner?"

Jan laughed. "Justin, you're actually a romantic." She reached over and kissed him lightly on the cheek. "But, I can't get involved with Brett or anyone else at this point in my life. I don't have time for a serious relationship—not now."

"You mean you don't want to take time for a relationship. If you genuinely cared for him, you'd make time in your life for him."

"So you're saying that I must not have real feelings for him, right?" she asked.

"That's how it looks to me, and that's how it probably looks to Brett, too," replied Justin.

Jan stared at her nephew for a few minutes before muttering, "But, unfortunately, I think I might have feelings for him."

"Well, you certainly haven't given him any hint that you might. It's no wonder that he just keeps riding away. How many times do you think he's going to reach out to you? Believe me, I wouldn't even have come back the second time."

"You're right. I haven't given him much reason to hang around, but I think he scares me."

"Scares you? I always thought you were fearless."

"Well, that just goes to show that you don't know me as well as you think you do. Anyway, I'm not sure why I'm even having this conversation with you." Jan reached out and put her arm around Justin's waist. "Let's get this amazing animal back to the barn for a nice rub down and the treat he deserves."

"Sure, dodge the real issues in life and bury yourself in Raven—real healthy, Aunt Jan."

"For gosh sakes, Justin, drop it. I'm fine, and I'll work out the Brett Kendall issue myself, eventually. Right now, I have to get back to the barn, grab something to eat, and then head over to the auditorium where the band is rehearsing. I promise that if we finish rehearsing at a decent hour, I'll give Brett a call. Satisfied?"

"Bet you ten bucks that you don't call him," mocked Justin, smiling at his aunt. "You really are a coward."

Jan turned away from Justin and pretended to be loosening the girth on her saddle. She knew that Justin was right—she was a coward when it came to Brett Kendall. She didn't know how to handle her feelings or his attempts at taking their relationship to

169

the next level. She had never thought or worried about establishing a relationship with the opposite sex. She simply hadn't met anyone that stirred the same emotions in her that he caused. *What would it hurt to have dinner with him just once more,* she wondered. *Perhaps it might even eliminate all the questions swirling through my mind. Maybe I would discover that I had no true interest in him after all.*

Chapter 23

The evening rehearsal lasted until well past midnight, and Jan was exhausted. She had completely forgotten about Brett Kendall as she worked with the band and her back-up singers on the new song. Roger had food catered in for them, and she had ravenously consumed a sub and some of the pizza. She was relaxed and thoroughly enjoying the camaraderie of the band and her road crew. They were a terrific group of people, who were tremendously talented and dedicated to her. *Strange*, she thought as she helped clear away some of the trash from their makeshift table, *when I'm with them, they seem like my family, and when I'm at the ranch that seems like home.*

"Do you want to run through the new song one more time before we leave," asked Roger. "I think the melody was perfect on the last go through, but maybe we should do it once more to make sure it's firm in everyone's mind."

Jan sighed and looked around at the others in her crew, who were obviously feeling the same level of exhaustion she felt. "No, I don't think so. I think we all have it exactly the way we want it. Let's just call it a night. We can go through it a couple of times tomorrow afternoon."

"You're the boss," said Roger. "If you're okay with it, then that's all I care about." Turning to the others, he yelled, "Okay, gang, that's it for tonight. See you back here at noon tomorrow."

Jan could see the relief in the musician's eyes as they quickly began to cover their instruments and head for the door. "Thanks, everyone," she called out.

"I really appreciate your extra help with the new song. See you tomorrow."

Roger drove her back to the hotel, and she collapsed into bed without even taking off her clothes. She kicked off her boots and curled up under the soft, down-filled coverlet, immediately dropping off to sleep.

~~~~~

It was almost eight the next morning when she finally rolled over and glanced at the clock. "Good grief," she said immediately jumping out of bed. "How could I have slept that long?"

She hopped into the shower and then dressed quickly. She had to pack and get her things sent over to the motor coach. She had hoped to go to the barn to say good-bye to Raven and her family before heading to the rehearsal and before she was whisked away after the concert to continue the road tour. *Roger clearly told everyone to let me sleep*, she decided. *I wish he'd consult me once in a while about these things. I have too much to do and too little time to get it all done.* She grabbed her suitcase and began throwing her stuff into it. Then, she grabbed her cell phone to call Jamie.

"Good morning, sleepy head," said Jamie when her aunt's name flashed across the screen of her cell phone. "What's up?"

"Where are you?" asked Jan.

"I'm downstairs in the lobby, waiting for you to call me. I'll be right up."

"Great," said Jan, sitting atop of her bulging suitcase and trying to zip it shut. "I want to run out to the barn before I leave."

"On my way," said Jamie. "Do you need help

172

with your bags?"

"That would be great. Thanks."

Jan had just finished zipping the last bag when Richard and Jamie knocked at the door. "Hey, you two," she said, giving them each a hug, which obviously startled Richard. Jan smiled when she noticed his embarrassment at being hugged. "Sorry about that, Richard. It's just that you've sort of become family this week."

"Aunt Jan," shrieked Jamie.

"Well, you'll have to admit, he certainly has experienced all of our dramas, and I think that qualifies him for a hug and a complementary membership into the Triple Bar Ranch family."

"I'm flattered," stammered Richard quickly grabbing one of the bags and putting it on the cart in the hall.

Jamie shot daggers at her, and Jan reached out to hug her. "Sorry," she whispered. "Now, let's talk schedule."

"Okay, shoot," answered Jamie. "What about breakfast for starters?"

"Don't have time. I want to go straight to the barn to say good bye to Raven, and then maybe we can all meet for lunch at the Café before I head over to the arena for rehearsal."

"Sounds almost right, but Roger will kill me if you tell him that you skipped breakfast. I have strict orders about making sure that you eat and rest before the rehearsal. No trauma; no disturbing situations; nothing to tire or upset you—I think that's how he explained how your day was to be spent. He even gave me money for a spa treatment for all four of us—mom, Beth, you and me. Please, please, can

173

we do that?"

Jan laughed. "Poor Roger, he's going to wear himself out if he thinks he can always keep me happy. Anyway, let's go to the barn first; and then we can talk about the spa treatment."

"Good, because I scheduled it for eleven and already told mom and Beth to meet us back here," said Jamie.

"It sounds like your day is going to be hectic, Miss Taylor," said Richard tossing Jan's last suitcase onto the cart. "I probably won't have a chance to see you again since you won't be coming back to the hotel. I just wanted to let you know what a privilege it was to meet you."

Jan reached out and gave him another hug. She laughed when he flinched again. "Hey, I'm sure I'll be seeing you again, so you'd better get used to the hugs. I'm a touchy, feely person who gives lots of hugs. Thanks so much for everything you did for me and for my family this week. You've been just great." She glanced around the room to make sure she had everything. "By the way, Richard, I left a ticket for you in will-call for the concert tonight. Are you going to be able to come?"

"Wouldn't miss it," responded Richard. "What you did for the Kirbys was really considerate. They can't wait to attend the concert."

Jan smiled and hugged him again. "I warned you," she said laughing. "Okay, Jamie, I think I have everything. We need to load the suitcases in the truck and then stop out at the show to transfer them to the motor coach. I guess this is it."

"*On the road again*," sang Jamie. "*I can't wait to get on the road again…*"

"That's a great song, but it's not exactly how I

feel," said Jan putting her arm around the shoulders of her niece as they headed for the elevator. "Personally, I can't wait to get off the road and get back home for the holidays."

After they had stopped at the motor coach, and Bill had put her bags inside, Jan and Jamie headed for the barn. When they got out of the truck, Jan stopped short. "That's Raven's whinny. Poor baby, he knows this is another goodbye," she said as she started running to the barn.

As soon as she turned the corner of the aisle leading to Raven's stall, he stopped whinnying and began to nicker softly. "Hey, Buddy," said Jan soothingly, "you need to stop all the ruckus. We'll both be home before you know it." She opened the stall door and pulled Raven's giant face toward her, kissing him on the bridge of his nose. For the next half-hour, she brushed and talked to Raven, promising him that she would be back to the ranch and that they would soon be streaming together across the ridge at sunset.

Raven stood quietly, listening to her gentle voice and nudging her with his head as she rubbed his body with a soft, lambs-wool cloth and softly sang her new song to him.

When it was time to leave, Jamie and Justin quietly approached the stall. They were both surprised to see tears in Jan's eyes as she looked over at them.

"Isn't this nuts?" sobbed Jan. "I absolutely hate to leave him. I think it's harder to leave him than it is you."

"Well, thanks a lot," said Justin entering the stall.

Jan reached out and gave him a hug as he

pulled out his handkerchief and started wiping the tears from her face.

"You know what I mean," she explained. "It's not that I don't hate to leave you too, but it's just that I know you guys understand that I'll be back, and I'm not sure that he understands that."

"Oh, I think he understands everything you say to him. He's not your typical horse—not by far," replied Jamie.

"Okay, Buddy. This is it," said Jan reaching up and hugging Raven once more around the neck. She kissed him on the cheek before turning around to leave the stall. As she slid the stall door closed, Raven let out one of the most mournful screams she had ever heard, causing the three of them to cover their ears. "Raven," yelled Jan. "Stop that. It's not good for you, and it makes me sad." Raven reared up and pawed the air, then immediately lay down in his stall.

"Here we go," moaned Justin. "Another week off food, and refusing to do anything. He's really a pill."

"Come on. Let's get out of here before I really start to bawl," said Jan dragging them away from the stall.

"So much for making sure you don't get upset today," moaned Jamie.

"Speaking of being upset," said Justin turning to Jan. "Did you make the call you promised to make last night?"

Jan reached in her jeans pocket and slapped ten dollars in Justin's outstretched hand.

"I knew you were a coward," he teased.

"No, I was exhausted, and it was after midnight when we finished. Besides, Roger brought in pizza and subs," she explained, shoving him with her hip. "Now, give me a hug and go away. We're off to a ladies afternoon of total indulgence without any male interference."

"Does all this have something to do with Brett Kendall?" asked Jamie.

"Forget it," said Jan. "See you tonight back stage," she called to Justin as she and Jamie climbed into the truck.

Chapter 24

Jan stood in front of the full-length mirror in the motor coach. For her first session of the show, she had chosen to wear a short, sea-green, sleeveless chiffon dress with a V-neckline accented with three rows of small crystals. The clear crystals scattered lightly all over the dress sparkled as she swayed back and forth in front of the mirror. The empire waist tastefully accented her full bust line and allowed the bottom of the dress to swing softly around her knees, The short skirt exposed her tanned, shapely legs and her hand-crafted tan and sea-green leather boots. The fullness of the dress provided plenty of unrestricted movement.

She was extraordinarily active on stage, and she picked her clothing to allow for maximum flexibility. Around her neck, she wore a silver choker with a large crystal studded cross dangling just above the point of the neckline on the dress. She wore the cross at every performance. It was a gift from her dad.

Tonight she decided to wear her hair down and let the natural curls fall as they would around her face. She opened the hatbox and placed her hat on an angle, slightly cocked to the right. A vibrant green band and a large rhinestone buckle off to the side were the only trim on the tan Stetson. She swirled around in the dress to make sure that the soft fabric didn't cling to her legs and that the skirt was long enough not to expose too much of her upper thighs.

Roger usually had the final say in the selection of her show wardrobe. He made certain that her outfits were tasteful because many of her fans were young women, and he wanted her to portray a classy, sexy look. The reporters who wrote about her performances typically described her as stylishly, seductive.

Satisfied with her appearance, she opened the door to her dressing area of the motor coach and walked out into the living area where Jan and Justin were waiting to walk over to the stage with her.

"You look gorgeous, Aunt Jan," gushed Jamie. "I love that dress. Do you think I could wear it to the Christmas dance?"

Jan laughed. "I don't see why not; we're about the same size. What do you think, Justin? Do you like this outfit?" she asked.

Justin just stared at her in awe. Finally, he cleared his throat and muttered, "It's hard to wrap my head around the fact that the person I'm staring at in that gorgeous, sexy outfit is actually my aunt who cleans stalls with me in her raggedy blue jeans, bulky flannel shirt, and scuffed up boots. Are you sure you're my aunt?"

"I'll take that as an approval," said Jan, pleased at their response to her appearance. "Okay. It's time to move out of here to the stage. Are y'all ready?"

They started for the door of the coach just as Roger opened it. "You look perfect," he said making a low-whistle sound. "That outfit ought to make them go wild, right off the bat."

"You're just saying that because you picked it out," teased Jan.

"I do have good taste, but it's your body that makes the dress," he said. "By the way, Melanie Kirby and all seven of her cousins decided they wanted to be out front instead of back stage, so they could get the whole experience of the concert. They're going to

179

be seated in section A off to your right about half-way back. You ready?"

"I'm ready," said Jan. She always got nervous right before a performance, but her tension disappeared the moment she stepped out on stage. The only thing she thought about then was how much fun it was to work with the band and to belt out the songs that she loved. She never got tired of singing the same songs because the audience was always so responsive to them, and she got her energy from them.

"Oh, my god, I couldn't get out there on that stage with all those people staring at me for anything in the world. I don't know how you do it?" muttered Jamie.

"Shush, Jamie," complained Justin, dragging her away from Jan. "You'll make her nervous. Break a leg, Aunt Jan. You're going to wow them with that outfit if nothing else," he called as he and Jamie darted behind the curtain to the other side of the stage.

When the band started playing her theme song, the crowd went nuts, and she stepped on the lift that raised her up to the top of a long staircase leading down to the front of the stage. Dozens of spotlights shined down on her through a misty fog and dancing lasers. It was a dramatic entrance, just the way Roger and the crowd wanted it to be. "Hello, Oklahoma," she yelled before starting her descent down the staircase. At the bottom of the stairs, she grabbed her guitar, and the band began the introduction to her favorite up-beat song called, *A Cowgirls Wish*. She smiled to herself as she realized that Roger had altered the lighting to let her see much more of the audience, especially those seated to the right of the stage. She immediately located Melanie and her cousins and waved to them.

The first two sessions of the performance went perfectly. The lighting had made all the difference in the world for her. She could interact with fans that followed her to most of her concerts and enjoyed watching them sing along to her songs.

Now, as she quickly slipped into the white floor length dress for her final appearance, she could feel the nervousness about her new song creeping over her. She quickly glanced in the small mirror in the makeshift dressing room behind stage hoping to gain some confidence from her appearance. The dress was new—one she had picked out specifically to introduce the new song. It was made of soft, white organza with a pleated, cowl neckline in front and a low, draped back accented with a large rhinestone buckle at the waistline. It was tightly fitted at the waist to accent her figure, and then it flowed out to a full skirt studded with clear crystals. Three rows of crystals encircled the edge of each of the wrist length sleeves. The front was split up the middle to just above her knees, allowing her high top, white leather boots to show and the full skirt to flow behind her as she walked.

Her hands were shaking as she transferred her cross on to a longer silver chain and slipped it over her head. She had decided not to wear a hat. Instead, she brushed her hair back on the right side and attached a large, silk gardenia in the back just behind her ear. Small diamond stud earrings sparkled in the pale light in the dressing room.

"Are you ready," whispered Roger through the curtain that served as the door to her dressing room.

"Ready," she said.

As she stepped out of the dressing room, Roger just stared in amazement.

"What?" said Jan. "Do you like it? I know you

didn't pick it out, but I think it fits the song, right?"

"You look like an angel," he muttered. "The outfit is perfect. The song is beautiful, and so are you. They're going to love it, and they already love you, so relax and enjoy the moment."

"I hope you're not just trying to make me feel good. I'm really nervous about this," she said as she stepped upon the platform that would lift her for the last time tonight to the top of the stage. "Here goes," she said as the band began to play the melody of her song.

Jan slowly descended the stairs to the rhythm of the song. Her skirt billowed behind her, and the crystals sparkled as the white spotlights swung back and forth across the stage. When she reached the bottom of the stairs, she walked down the extended runway and gracefully sat on the stool at the end. She bowed her head slightly for a moment then introduced the song. "I want to close tonight's performance with a special song that I wrote for a very dear, young friend, Melanie Kirby." A spotlight swung over to shine on Melanie who meekly smiled and waved. "Melanie's family is facing some tough times as her older sister continues to battle cancer. The words of my song come from something my dad used to say to me when I was upset about things that were not the way I thought they should be. I know the song is a lot different from any of my other hits, but I hope you like it." She then turned toward Melanie and whispered in the mike, "Melanie, sweetheart, this song's for you." The lights went off in the auditorium except for one overhead spot that shined down on Jan. She drew in a deep breath and then began to sing the words.

~~~~~~

One day when I was just a child,

I climbed on daddy's knee.
No matter what I thought was wrong,
He'd make it right for me.

"What's wrong today, my tiny child,"
He asked and held me tight.
"Please tell me all about it,
And I'll try to make it right."

I asked why bad things happen,
To people who are good,
And asked why things don't seem to go,
The way I think they should.

He sat real still for just awhile,
And then he sang to me,
A song that I still sing today,
When life's a mystery.

Keep your eyes on Heaven,
You don't need to know why.
Keep your eyes on Heaven,
And you'll know by and by.

Keep your eyes on Heaven,
Put your trust in God's hand.
Keep your eyes on Heaven,
He has a plan.

Keep your eyes on Heaven.

~~~~~

As she started to sing the chorus, she could see
her fans waving the light from cell phones that glowed

like candles in the dark. When she finished the song, the auditorium was silent. Suddenly, a soft clap began as Melanie Kirby stood and started clapping her tiny hands together. The applause then grew until it was the loudest and longest round of applause Jan could ever remember receiving. As she began climbing up the stairs, the band played the chorus again, and the audience sang the words. Jan was thrilled—she had accomplished her goal. Melanie had obviously heard the message, and the audience easily remembered the melody and words of the song. When she reached the top of the stairs, she turned and waved, calling out, "I love you Oklahoma." A light mist and a bright light hid her slow descent behind the stage.

From his place in the front row of the second tier of seats, Brett smiled at the beautiful scene below him. He knew now, without any doubt, that he was truly in love with Jan Taylor. A lump formed in his throat as she slowly disappeared into the fog. *How can I just walk away from her? I can't. I won't,* he proclaimed.

Chapter 25

As the motor coach pulled away from the World Show, she scanned the crowd swarming around it for Brett, but she didn't see him. She wondered if he had even been at the show. She watched out the tinted windows as her sisters and Jamie and Justin slipped out of sight. After being with them this week, she realized that she would miss them even more until she finally got back home.

Roger was so excited about how well the new song had been received that he was beside himself. "We need to get that out on a CD right away," he said. "The audience obviously loved it."

"If we do cut a single of the song, I want at least half of the proceeds to go into a foundation for the Kirbys," replied Jan. "After all, they were the inspiration for it."

"That's fine by me," replied Roger. "I'll get the accountants on it right away. Now, let's celebrate," he said popping open a can of Dr. Pepper.

"Not before I get out of this dress," responded Jan, heading to the back of the motor coach.

When she had changed into her jeans and old flannel shirt, Roger laughed as she came out of her living quarters. "The princess has just transitioned back into Cinderella," he said, handing her a can of soda. "To you," he said, tipping his can toward her, "and to your new hit."

For the next several hours, they talked about Jan's future, and Roger laid out his plans to satisfy

185

her desire to reduce the amount of travel she had to make to record her songs and to rehearse new shows. They agreed that the best place for a recording studio and rehearsal hall would be in Luchenbach, Texas, which was just a thirty-minute drive from the gate of the Three Bar Ranch.

"By building it in Luchenbach, it could serve some of the other great country stars from Texas, making it more profitable for the investor," explained Roger. "And, you would still be able to go home every night after a recording session or rehearsal. What do you think?"

"It sounds almost too good to be true," said Jan. She walked to the fridge to grab a handful of grapes. Leaning against the door of the refrigerator, she asked, "When do I get to find out where all the venture capital for this recording studio is coming from?"

"Why do you need to know who your angel supporter is? Just be glad that you have someone out there willing to invest in you and in the future of country music."

"Someone? Are we talking about one investor?" she asked.

Roger shifted uneasily in the big leather recliner. "Right now, I only have one investor, and I think he prefers to do this alone."

"He?" she pried.

"Come on, Jan. He made me promise that he would remain anonymous. Look, it's a fantastic offer. He intends to be a silent partner, letting us run the whole thing. You rarely find a deal like that. He's also willing to let you buy him out at any point you want to."

"Hmm," said Jan. "That kind of offer sounds

vaguely familiar. It sounds a lot like the offer that Brett Kendall made to some of the ranchers. Please tell me that he isn't my Secret Angel."

"I'm not going to tell you who it is or who it isn't, so if this is all going to happen for you, you need to stop asking me questions. Okay?"

Jan stared at him for a long time, and then finally muttered, "Okay, no more questions. If you don't mind then, I'm going to turn in. I really am tired." She walked over to Roger and leaned over to give him a kiss on the cheek. "I trust you, my dear future brother-in-law. I really do appreciate the whole plan and everything you and some mysterious person are doing to give me the better of two worlds."

"You're worth investing in, Jan. You really do have a promising future, and I would never do anything to sacrifice that. I promise you this is a great opportunity for you."

"It's not too bad a deal for you either," Jan teased. "You'll be a lot closer to Beth too."

"Hmm, I was afraid you would eventually discover my real motive for this whole thing." He laughed and hugged her tightly. "I do love that woman and naturally want to be as close to her as I can for as much time as possible."

"Well, this sounds like a win-win for both of us. Thanks for everything, Roger. And, by the way, thanks for the different lighting tonight. I could see more of the audience, and it makes performing a lot more personal and enjoyable." She smiled and opened the door to her sleeping quarters.

"Love ya," said Roger. "Sleep tight."

~~~~~

The next week flew by in a maze of travel,

visits to local country music stations in small and large cities they passed through on their way to Albuquerque's new Sandia Casino, and in rehearsals. Jan and Roger decided to keep the show as it was before the Oklahoma performance rather than to include her new song as the closing act. But, when she came out to do her final curtain call at the end of the Albuquerque performance, some of her fans began to chant, "*Keep Your Eyes On Heaven.*"

The reporters who followed her performances had been so impressed with the song and the story behind it that they had written about it in *Billboard* and on the *GAC* (Great American Country) and *CMT* websites. Her fan club blogged about it too, so news about the song traveled throughout the country music world. Her Albuquerque fans obviously wanted to hear the song, so she sang it for them as her final encore request. Once again, when she began to sing the chorus, they waved their cell phones like candles, and there was a brief hush as the last notes of the song faded away. The momentary silence was then followed by a burst of applause that shook the lights in the new theater.

The following day, when they arrived in Phoenix, reporters swarmed her motor home as they pulled into the Celebrity Theater parking lot. Roger looked out the side window of the motor home. "I'll take care of setting up a news conference for you," he said to Jan. "Just stay put in here for a while."

Jan could hear Roger fielding questions about the new song and arranging for a news conference during their first sound check rehearsal. He was a master at handling the media, and she was truly grateful. When he came back on the bus, he was all smiles and exuberance. "I've arranged for all of them to attend the sound-check rehearsal this afternoon and promised that you would sing the new song for them. Is that all right?" he asked.

188

"Whatever you say—you're the media boss, but I don't want to expose the Kirby's to a lot of unwanted attention. We need to make the media understand that and to encourage reporters and the paparazzi to respect the Kirby's privacy. Maybe I should call Mr. Kirby before this all gets out of hand."

"I already called them the other night after you went to bed when we left Oklahoma. Mr. Kirby said they had already been contacted by reporters and offers to help with expenses. He was actually grateful, but I contacted a media specialist in Little Rock and hired her to protect them from too much invasion of their privacy."

"You're a saint," said Jan. "I still think I want to call them and offer my own apology for any difficulties that this has created for them. I just didn't think about causing a media frenzy or making their life any more difficult than it already is. What about Melanie, is she still in Oklahoma?"

"She is, but Mr. Kirby said his sister-in-law is prepared. According to him, she's like a wild-cat when it comes to protecting her children, so he isn't worried that anyone will be getting too close to Melanie."

"Good for her," said Jan. "I think that's how I would be if I ever have children of my own."

When Roger left to arrange for the rehearsal, Jan placed the call to Mr. Kirby. She was relieved when he reassured her that they were grateful to her for all the offers of assistance that they were receiving. He was especially delighted about a new van that one of the local dealerships had donated to them. The van was equipped with a lift and other special features to allow them to transport Jamie between home and the hospital when and if she could travel. The only fear he had was that the hospital might become concerned about the number of people trying to get to Jamie. She assured him that, in her future performances, she would not specifically identify them by name and that the media specialist Roger had hired would keep the visitors to the hospital under control.

She hung up the phone amazed at the generosity of strangers like the man who had donated the van and about how one little song could have such widespread consequences. In the past, she had sometimes complained about how invasive the media was, but this time she actually appreciated their help in getting the Kirby story told in places where it would make a difference in their lives.

After the sound check rehearsal, she and Roger decided to change the closing of her performance back to the way she had done it in Oklahoma. But, in keeping with her commitment to Mr. Kirby, she would not specifically identify them as her inspiration for the song.

Her last concert on the tour was at Fair Park in Dallas, which was one of her favorite places to perform. This time it was even more important to her because it was her last stop before heading back to the Three Bars Ranch.

Through daily texts and emails, Jamie had kept her up-to-date on all the family doings and about Raven. According to Jamie, Raven had pouted for several days, but finally had begun to eat and to be his rebellious self again once they got him back to the ranch.

Yesterday, Jamie had called her from the barn, so she could listen to Raven's hideous screams.
"He knows you're near," Jamie had reported. "He started this screaming last night and is pacing around in his stall so much that we're going to put him out in

his paddock today and leave him there until you get home."

That night, as Roger was walking with her from the motor home to the stage, she looked over at him and said, "One more concert and then home. I can't wait," she called out as the lift began to raise her to the top of the stage in her sea-green dress.

"Me too," called Roger. "By tomorrow night, you'll be soaring over the ridge chasing the sunset with that crazy horse of yours, and I'll finally be back with my beautiful artist. Life really is good."

Jan smiled and tipped her hat to him just as she reached the top of the stage staircase. She stared at the huge audience in front of her and yelled out, "Hello, fellow Texans!"

~~~~~

The next morning after the Dallas performance, Jan was up before dawn. She threw on her jeans and flannel shirt and headed out to the living quarters to wake up Roger. She was surprised when she opened her door to find his bed already made up and fresh coffee brewing in the coffee pot. "He's obviously even more anxious than I am to get home." She looked out the window of the motor home and saw him coming across the grounds at Fair Park with a box of donuts.

"Good morning," he said as he hopped up the steps of the motor home. "You ready?" he asked. "I thought we'd just have some donuts on the road rather than taking the time to find a place to eat. That way we'll be home in time for a good ol' Texas noon time dinner."

"Sounds perfect. Is Bill okay with that?" she asked.

"He's been up and ready for hours. Don't

191

forget that he's probably as anxious to get back home for the holidays as we are."

"I'm sure he is," said Jan. She knew that everyone associated with the tour was glad to be heading home for a while. Last night, they had all celebrated the end of the tour together, and Roger had announced the potential plans for the recording and rehearsal hall in Luchenbach.

Most of the band and singers were thrilled because they lived somewhere in Texas, but some of them were concerned because their homes were in Nashville or in Branson, Missouri where she had done most of her recording in the past. She was afraid she might lose a couple of her band members but hoped they would at least consider staying on.

She had watched Roger single out those who would be most affected by the change in location. She knew that they were under contract with her for at least one more year, but she would never hold them to their contract if they truly didn't want to come to Texas for a major portion of the year. The principal members of the band—the lead guitarist, key board player, and drummer—were all from Texas and were ecstatic over the news. Her lead back-up singers were also excited because they too were scattered across Texas.

Jan liked everyone associated with her show, including the roadies and stage crew that traveled with them, and she hated changing the dynamics of their close group. But, she selfishly wanted to lessen her own travel for recording sessions and rehearsals, and this was the possibility that promised to let her live in both of her preferred worlds. She just hoped that the probable changes to her band and crew would not ultimately change the culture of their group.

~~~~~

After the nearly five-hour trip from Dallas, the motor-home finally rolled into the long lane that led back to the ranch. Jan smiled at the big welcome home sign and balloons that decorated the iron gate across the main entrance. "I'll get out and key in the access code," she called to Bill and Roger.

As she stepped out of the coach, she could instantly hear Raven's wild whinnies echoing across the pasture. She quickly typed in the access code and motioned for the coach to drive through the gate. She then typed the code in once more to close the gate behind them. As she hopped back inside the coach, she instructed Bill to stop at the next paddock area. "See just ahead of you," she said pointing out the front window. "That's Raven's paddock, and I want to get out there."

As the coach drew nearer to his paddock, Raven raced toward the fence along the driveway. "Stop," Jan yelled to Bill. She threw open the door of the coach before it had come to a complete stop and jumped out, racing across the lane to where Raven was nervously prancing back and forth. She climbed the rail fence and threw both arms around his massive neck. Raven immediately stopped the hideous screaming as Jan climbed on his back.

Bill and Roger watched in amazement as she and Raven sailed across the pasture toward the barn where Jamie and Justin were waiting for them. "If that horse hurts her, I'll shoot him " moaned Roger. "Just look at them. They're flying across that rough ground like someone racing for a win at the Kentucky Derby."

"I don't think you'll ever have to worry about that horse hurting her," said Bill. "I think he'd fight anything or anyone that dared to attempt harming her."

Chapter 26

Jan was relieved to be home. As she walked to the barn that evening, she felt as if she had never been away. *Funny*, she mused, *coming home seems to instantly erase the memories of the hassle of travelling and the strange disconnectedness that I feel when I'm away.*

Lacey and Jim had a homecoming celebration for her. It was an old-fashioned western barbecue complete with thick, juicy steaks cooked to perfection over an open pit of smoldering embers of seasoned wood. Several of her friends from nearby ranches were there, but Brett wasn't. She wondered why. Surely, he had been invited. She hadn't asked about him because she didn't want to arouse any suspicions about her feelings for him. *Maybe he has gone back to Kentucky,* she thought. *I hope not.* During the past several weeks on her tour, she thought about him constantly and couldn't wait to see him again. She knew now that the mixed feelings she felt toward him were simply because, for the first time in her life, she felt vulnerable. She had always been sure of herself—confident that she could handle any situation, but once he appeared in her life, she became unsure of what to do, what to say, and simply how to be herself. *I have actually fallen in love with him. I realize that now. So, what do I want to do about it,* she wondered. *This is all new territory for me. I have no idea how to tell him how I feel or what to expect from him.*

As she approached the barn, she could hear Raven start to nicker. He knew that it was almost time for their evening ride. She looked up at the rays of the sinking, evening sun bouncing off the shiny metal roof of the main horse barn.

Various types and styles of barns were scattered across the vast acreage of the ranch. Pole barns of various sizes provided shelter for cattle and pasture horses. Others were western style, storage barns used to store hay and grain, but her favorite barn was the main horse barn that was in the center of several smaller barns used for breeding, birthing, and housing horses. Like the barns on most western ranches, their horse barns were positioned to take advantage of the prevailing winds of the area to ensure the best air quality for the horses and to protect the barns from the extreme weather conditions that are part of the climate of Texas. The dormer windows on the roof of the main barn flooded the interior with light and fresh air.

The exterior of the main barn was made of old stone. It was built years ago by her great, great grandparents and had stood the tests of time and use. Inside the main barn, eight stalls lined each side of a wide center aisle. Huge doors opened on both ends of the barn allowing fresh air to blow through it. The doors also served as possible quick exits in the case of fire, which is a major worry to every horse owner. Each stall also had a rear Dutch door along the outside wall, allowing the horses to socialize and to enjoy the view and the early morning and evening breezes. A small overhang ran along the entire length of each side of the barn to protect the horses from direct sun and the other elements of Texas weather.

Inside the barn, the walls between the stalls were high, intended to provide the horses protection from one another and to allow them to relax while they ate without fear of interference. Arched openings in the front of the stalls allowed the horses to stick their heads out into the aisle and to see one another. Horses are gregarious animals and don't like to be

195

totally isolated.

At the end of the row of stalls, there were three large tack stalls and a heated wash stall for bathing the horses. A hallway off the main aisle lead to a small apartment and office complex. During fouling and breeding seasons, Jan often lived in the apartment. Outside of the office complex were large, glass cases to display the numerous ribbons, trophies, and other awards won by the Triple Bar Ranch horses and their riders.

As she entered the cavernous barn, she stopped at Raven's stall to pat him. "Hang in there, fellow," she said. "I just want to check on things in my office, then we'll head out to catch the sun."

As she opened the door to her office, she drew in a deep breath. *Home*, she thought. *I'm finally home.* Her office used to be her father's office and was the largest of three offices in the barn. Jim and Lacey occupied the other two. She plopped down in the soft leather, swivel chair behind her huge, walnut desk. She leaned the chair back and began to think about all the changes that had happened in the lives of her family in just the short three weeks since they had been together at the World Show. She was relieved to learn that Lacey had discovered that high stress was the cause of her health problems, but now that she and Jim were going to be married Thanksgiving weekend, most of the tension in her life would be lessened.

She was somewhat surprised to discover that Richard Evans was already completing his internship at the Kendall ranch and overseeing some of their own breeding operations. Jamie was delighted, of course, especially since she had been accepted by an online Veterinarian program that would allow her to do most of her studying from home with the exception of one weekend a month that she would spend at a local college and the clinical experiences she would complete at the local Veterinarian Hospital. Lacey had confided to Jan that she was certain that Jamie would be sporting an engagement ring after Christmas—an anticipated gift, naturally from Richard.

Beth had already set things in motion for a New Years Eve wedding for her and Roger. She was also amazed that Beth had taken an instrumental role in setting up all of the contacts for the new recording studio that Roger had asked her to arrange. Beginning tomorrow morning, Roger would be meeting with realtors, architects, and local contractors to get all of the plans, licenses and approvals required for the new studio. Beth had presented her with a beautiful rendering of the studio and rehearsal hall that she had painted herself.

I can't believe that I can actually have a singing career and still continue to pursue my passion for training and caring for horses. She sighed and looked out the large window in her office. Glancing upward, she muttered, "Thank you."

Justin lightly tapped on the door of her office and stuck his head around the corner. "I thought I would find you out here. Are you glad to be home?"

Jan smiled at him. "You have no idea how much I am thrilled to be back here." She stared at him for a moment, and then asked, "How are you feeling about all the changes going on around here?"

"Do you mean about mom and Jim getting married?" he asked.

"Yeah, that, and the possibility of Jamie getting engaged to Richard."

"I'm cool with it all," he said. "I'm glad for mom, and I know Jim is the person that dad would have

197

chosen to take his place. I still miss him, though," he mumbled, dropping his head.

"We all do," whispered Jan. "But you know he's always with us in our hearts and in our thoughts."

Justin sat silently, staring out of the window at the setting sun. "Well, I guess I'd better get out of here and let you head out with your wild beast to chase the sun across the ridge."

"It's that time of the day," she said, pushing back from the desk. "I'd ask you to come with us, but it's sort of our thing. You don't mind, do you?"

"Actually, I do mind," said Justin, "but not because I want to go with you. It's dangerous. What if you'd fall off or something? Do you even take your cell phone with you?"

"If I needed help, I'm sure Raven would let you know. His wild screams are more dependable than a cell phone out there," answered Jan. "Quit worrying. We've been doing this for years, and we've always come back safe and sound. Raven knows the path across the top of that ridge so well he could run it blindfolded. All I do is hang on and enjoy the thrill of the ride. I love it."

Justin followed her out of the office to Raven's stall. "Don't forget, part of that ridge is owned by Brett Kendall now, not us. It's part of that piece of land he bought from mom."

Jan was surprised that she no longer felt angry about the mention of Brett's purchase of some of their property. "Well, we'll just make sure he hasn't put up any fences between the properties. That ridge belongs to Raven and me," she said.

Justin gave her a leg up onto Raven's back. "Why don't you use a saddle or a bridle on these crazy rides?" he asked.

198

"Because I want Raven to feel as free as I do." she said grabbing hold of Raven's mane and galloping full speed out of the barn. "See you in a bit," she called.

Chapter 27

Brett wondered how Jan's homecoming celebration went. He wanted to be there, but he had agreed with Jim that it was important for the two ranches to have some representation at the ranchers' meeting, so he had volunteered to attend. It turned out to be a good thing that he had gone to the meeting because he had learned about a threat to the security of cattle and young horses for all the ranches in the area. According to Bill Fletcher, a huge cougar had killed several of his calves and one of his prized yearlings during the past month. Several of the other ranchers had also lost livestock and reported that they had spotted the large cat above the ridge that ran along the southern border of the Three Bar Ranch and his property. Bill told the group that he and his boys had tracked the cat to what they believed to be its den at the top of the ridge but had been unable to get a shot at it. At the meeting, they all agreed to conduct a hunting party tomorrow morning to find the cougar before it struck again.

He glanced at his watch—*too late now to head over to the Taylors*, he decided. As he hopped out of his utility vehicle and headed to the barn to open the door so he could park the ATV inside, an insidious roar unexpectedly echoed across the valley. It was the fierce roar of a cougar, and it sounded close by. He stood still, frozen in his tracks with his hand on the barn door listening to the beastly roar. Then, he heard a second, more familiar sound—the horrific scream of a horse. As the two sounds continued to destroy the tranquility of the peaceful evening, he suddenly realized that he recognized the high-pitched whinny. It was Raven. The familiar whinny continued repeatedly like a desperate call for help. "Oh, my god," he shouted. "Jan must have gone out riding across the ridge." He tried to run back toward the ATV, but his feet felt like they were stuck in wet cement. It was only with considerable strength and determination that he was able to move at all.

When he finally got to the ATV, he quickly reached behind the seat to make sure his rifle was there and simultaneously slammed his foot down on the accelerator, speeding off toward the ridge and the horrific screams and roars that continued to fill the silence of the night.

~~~~~

Justin had just returned to the patio to enjoy the barbecue with the rest of his family when, without warning, the echo of Raven's recognizable scream began reverberating among the outbuildings of the ranch. He shot up out of his chair so fast that it tipped over backward, and he had to jump over it as he ran toward the barn. Jamie and Richard followed him in close pursuit. When he reached the barn, he grabbed the hackamore from the hock outside of his gelding's stall and quickly threw it over the nose of his horse. He leaped onto the horse's back and galloped full speed out of the stall. "Get the first-aid kits," he yelled as he rode past Jamie and Richard. As he flew past the patio, he yelled at his mom to call the hospital and have them start the medical-helicopter toward the ridge.

He leaned over the withers of his horse urging him to go faster and faster. In the distance, he could see the headlights of an ATV racing toward the ridge and assumed that Brett Kendall had also heard the heinous sounds. As Justin urged his horse across the top of the ridge, Raven's screams grew louder and louder and were mixed with the guttural growl and roar of a cougar. He could feel the tension in his own horse as he urged him to continue to gallop toward the sounds.

The moon suddenly slipped behind the ridge and darkness spread out across the valley. Justin continued to race his horse blindly through the dim light until he could finally make out the silhouette of Raven rearing and striking out at something. There was no sign of Jan. He raced his horse toward the headlights of the ATV and was shocked when he saw Brett leap from the small truck with a rifle. "Don't shoot," yelled Justin, catapulting from the back of his horse and stumbling across the rocky terrain at the foot of the ridge as he raced toward Brett.

"For gods sake, Justin," yelled Brett. "I'm not going to shoot Raven, it's that damned cougar I want to get."

Brett pointed the rifle toward the cougar. "Dammit," he yelled, "I can't get a clear shot without taking the risk of hitting Raven." The two men watched in horror as the large cat tore at Raven's front legs each time he lowered them to the ground, but Raven continued to charge the cougar repeatedly. He reared and struck out courageously while the vicious cougar constantly swiped at him with his malicious claws. Finally, Raven struck the depraved cougar with a thunderous blow to its head, and the horrid animal immediately stopped its beastly growls and fell motionless beneath the continued pounding of Raven's powerful hooves.

In the light from the headlights on Brett's ATV, Justin could see the glint of the wet streams of blood running down Raven's side from the deep claw marks across his withers, and he stared in horror at the gushing blood coming from a deep gash on Raven's right foreleg. He jumped up from the ground and began walking slowly toward Raven. "Easy fellow," he called. "Easy Raven, we just want to help you."

Brett grabbed Justin and pulled him aside as Raven charged at him rearing and striking out with his injured leg. "He's out of control," warned Brett. "He's not going to let you touch him. We've got to find Jan. Can you see her anywhere?" Brett scanned the top of the ridge with the beam of a large flashlight.

"There," shouted Justin. "There she is, over there just behind Raven."

They both stared in horror at Jan's twisted, still body. Justin stood up again and began to run toward her, but Raven quickly darted in front of her body and charged at him again with teeth barred and ears plastered tightly against his head.

Brett rushed forward and once again dragged Justin away from the menacing attack of the distraught horse. "He's not going to let us near her," Brett yelled. "What do you want me to do?" he asked, grabbing his rifle.

"No," screamed Jamie's voice from the darkness. "Don't shoot him, please." She leaped from their ATV and began slipping and sliding up the side of the ridge toward them. She rushed past the two men and headed directly toward Raven, softly whistling and talking to him. "Easy, Raven," she whispered. "Jan needs us to help her. Please, let us help her." Tears streamed down her cheeks as she noticed the blood gushing down Raven's right foreleg. "You need some help too, Raven. Please."

She continued to creep slowly toward him, staying low so as not to be a threat to him. As she got almost close enough to touch him, he suddenly reared and charged at her, sending her tumbling backward down the ridge. She immediately jumped up and screamed out at him. "Stop it Raven. I mean it. Stop it right now. This is ridiculous," she shouted as she walked toward him with her arm outstretched and holding a peppermint in her hand. "Settle down right this minute, Raven," she screeched.

As she approached the wild horse without any sign of fear, Raven stopped his constant screaming and slowly limped toward her, gobbling the peppermint from her hand. Jamie immediately bent down and placed her hand over the spot on his leg where the blood was pouring out of a deep wound. "It's okay," she called calmly to the others. Just come quietly and stay low. Hurry, Richard," she cried. "He's going to bleed to death if we don't get this bleeding stopped."

Justin and Brett raced quickly toward Jan. Brett immediately placed his fingertips on the side of her neck. "Her heartbeat is strong," he said as tears gushed from his eyes. He quickly wiped them away with the back of his hand.

"Don't move her," called Richard. He had begun trying to clean Raven's wounds on his withers with a saline solution from the first-aid kit while Jamie continued to apply pressure to stop the bleeding on his leg.

"Stay with her," Brett shouted to Justin. He raced back to his ATV and grabbed the mike of his CB radio. In the distance, he heard the whirling sound of the medical helicopter and saw the bright search light scanning across the ridge. He realized that apparently someone had already notified the hospital. He dropped the mike and jumped into the ATV heading it to a flat area a short distance from where Jamie and Richard were trying to keep Raven calm. He quickly ripped off the cap of a flare and stood on the seat of the ATV, frantically waving the flare in the air. Within seconds, the helicopter headed toward him and began to lower itself slowly to the ground. As two of the medics jumped from the copter, Brett yelled,

"We need a backboard."

The two medics followed Brett up the rocky ridge to where Jan was lying. She was still unconscious. As they approached her, Raven raised his head and screamed wildly. Richard quickly grabbed the lead line they had tossed around his neck. He tried to calm Raven by stroking his cheek and softly whispering in his ear, but Raven continued to whinny loudly, straining against the rope and dragging Richard toward Jan. Jamie had no choice but to let loose of his leg causing the blood once again to rush out of the wound. She grabbed on to the lead rope and tried to help Richard restrain Raven, but he easily dragged them both to where the medics were frantically checking Jan's vitals. Towering above the medics, Raven began to paw the ground nervously with the injured leg. Jamie quickly grabbed it and again tried to apply pressure over the wound as he tugged and jumped around on his hind legs. "Whoa, Raven," she shouted repeatedly.

Brett kept an eye on Raven as the medics examined Jan. "It's okay," he said as one of the medics nervously glanced over at the menacing horse. "They have him under control," he said trying to sound convincing. As he looked down at Jan's pale face, he spotted blood trickling from behind her head. He glanced up at the medic with a look of sheer panic.

"It's probably only a flesh wound or a small cut from the fall," assured the medic. "We obviously need to move her away from that crazy horse, though. We're going to need you and Justin to help us keep her head and shoulders straight as we lift her onto the backboard."

"Right," shouted Justin who appeared to be holding himself together better than Brett was.

"On three," shouted the medic trying to be heard above Raven's continued screams. "One, two, three." They carefully slid Jan on to the wooden stretcher, and the medics immediately began to secure her head and body tightly to it so that she wouldn't slip or move as they carried her down the slope to the helicopter.

As they lifted her and headed down the mountain, Raven reared and screamed so mournfully that the medics froze in place. They turned to face the giant horse that was snorting and pawing the ground behind them. Justin and Brett stepped between the medics and Raven. "Go ahead, slowly," whispered Justin to the medics.

"No, Raven," shouted Jamie yanking on the rope around his neck. He lunged forward and jerked the rope out of her hands. "No," she shouted running out in front of him and waving her arms over her head. "They have to take Jan. She needs their help," she screamed.

Richard ran toward Jamie to help her by grabbing hold of the lead rope, but Raven reared again and began to drag him down the ridge toward the medics. Justin, Jamie, and Brett ran out in front of Raven frantically waving their arms and finally forcing him to stop. Before Raven could turn to go the other way, Richard was able to get to his feet and Brett quickly threw another rope that he had brought back with him from his ATV around Raven's neck. Justin and Jamie quickly grabbed hold of the rope, trying with all their strength to hold Raven back. Suddenly, Raven jerked his head up toward the night sky and screamed one more piercing whinny. He then slowly dropped to the ground, pitifully nickering with a tear trickling from his wild, defeated eyes.

Richard quickly scrambled to his feet and grabbed hold once again of the bleeding leg. "Jamie," he yelled. "Get the vet on the CB. Hurry, we've got to get this leg stitched and get some antibiotics in him right away before it's too late."

Brett turned around to see Justin sliding quickly down the ridge running to catch up with the medics. *Good*, he thought, *at least someone will be with Jan in case she wakes up during the flight to the hospital.* Then turning back to Richard, he yelled, "I have what you need to stitch up the wound in a medical kit in my ATV. "I'll get it."

"Hurry," Richard responded. "Just get me something quick or this horse is going to bleed to death."

Brett slid down the side of the ridge and raced toward the ATV. He got there just as the medics were loading Jan into the helicopter.

"Who's going with us in the copter," yelled the medic. "We only have room for one."

"Justin, you go. I'm sure she'd rather see your face than mine should she wake up during the flight."

"I'm not so sure about that," replied Justin, "but thanks. I hate to leave her."

Brett smiled as Justin reached out to give him a quick hug before racing away and jumping into the helicopter. He watched as the helicopter slowly lifted from the ground and then quickly darted across the valley toward the hospital in town. Remembering Richard's warning about the possibility of Raven bleeding to death, he quickly turned the ATV around and headed back toward Richard and Jamie, praying silently that both Jan and Raven would survive.

Chapter 28

Justin hovered over Jan's hospital bed, holding on to and gently stroking her hand. According to the doctors who examined her, she didn't appear to have any injuries other than a small cut on the back of her head and a severe concussion. The doctor's primary concern was that she remained unconscious indicating the possibility of a more serious head injury and the potentiality of permanent brain damage. Although the CT scan showed no indications of bruising or bleeding of the brain, the doctors had told Justin they were going to order an MRI later this morning just to get a closer look at the brain and surrounding tissue.

He leaned his head against the railing on the hospital bed and tried to think about the happy times he had shared with his Aunt. He was exhausted and emotionally drained. Gradually, he drifted off to a restless sleep.

When Brett entered the hospital room, he was glad to see Jan resting so peacefully. She looked like a pale angel with a halo of red hair encircling her head. Not wanting to disturb Justin, even though he looked terribly uncomfortable leaning against the metal railing, he quietly sat a huge bouquet of gardenias down on the nightstand and slipped out of the room.

He had stayed out all night on the ridge with Jamie, Richard, the vet and others who had gathered there to keep watch over Raven. They had to keep Raven where he was because they were afraid to move him until they were confident that the stitches would hold and that the bleeding was controlled. When the vet had arrived at the ridge, he complimented Richard on his careful cleaning and stitching of Raven's wounds, but warned if they tried to move him right away that the pressure of the bleed might rupture again, and Raven would more than likely bleed to death before they could reach the Vet hospital. He gave Raven pain shots and a tranquilizer to help him relax as well as a dose of strong antibiotics to fight off the possibility of infection.

Lacey and Jim had brought them blankets, sleeping bags, and food and water. Brett and Jim built a campfire, and they had all huddled around it keeping a watchful eye all night on Raven for any signs of fever or chills. They put several blankets over him to keep away the chill of the night air, and Jamie curled up beside him in her sleeping bag. She gently rubbed his muzzle and face and finally fell asleep with her arm draped over his massive neck.

Raven had not moved since he had succumbed earlier. It hurt Brett to see the fire gone from his soul, but he knew there was nothing that any of them could do to console him. Only Jan could do that.

As the word traveled across the ranchers CB network, several of them rode out to bring the group more food, coffee, and blankets. They dug a deep trench and buried the cougar to keep away any other predators. To a stranger, the peaceful scene would probably look like a simple, campfire gathering of friends and neighbors. The only sound across the valley now was an occasional howl from a lone coyote, the hoot of an owl, and the soft hum of conversation around the campfire.

Beth, Roger, and Justin had kept them informed

of Jan's progress at the hospital through a daisy chain of cell phones and CB radios. At daybreak, Brett had decided to head for the hospital himself. When he got there, he bribed the receptionist at the information desk to open the gift shop, so he could grab the bouquet of gardenias.

Now, as he left the hospital, instead of driving to his ranch, he decided that he would head back out to the ridge to see if they needed any help moving Raven this morning. Then, he would head home to shower and shave and go back to the hospital to relieve Justin.

As he pulled the ATV to a stop next to where they had been camping, he could tell by the tears streaming down Jamie's face that the news wasn't good. Raven's temperature had spiked in the last few hours indicating infection was spreading throughout his body. Though they tried to get him into the trailer, he had simply refused to move. "Don't you have some way to lift him," Brett asked of the vet.

"I've sent for another trailer that has the equipment to lift and load him. If we don't get him to the Vet hospital soon, so we can administer strong, intravenous antibiotics, he won't survive. But, honestly, I'm not even sure that the infection is the main concern here. It's as if he has decided he doesn't want to live. He refuses to move or drink or eat anything. I don't have any way to treat that type of deep depression. If he has given up on life, he'll surely die no matter what we do."

Jamie was cradling Raven's head in her lap, pleading with him to get up, but he refused even to open his eyes. Brett suddenly whirled around and yelled, "I'll be right back," he called as he sped toward the barn.

Within minutes, he had returned with a CD of

210

Jan's voice blasting from a portable CD player. He purposefully hid the ATV behind a clump of bushes so that Raven couldn't see where the voice was coming from. At the sound of Jan's voice, Raven opened his eyes and quietly nickered.

Jamie immediately began to urge him to get up. "Come on, Raven, let's go find Jan," she said. "Come on, baby. Jan wants to see you." As she continued to encourage Raven to get up, Brett slowly backed the ATV, moving it closer to the Vet's huge trailer.

Slowly, Raven raised his head. "Come on, Raven. You can do this for Jan. Get up, fellow," said Jamie, who was shaking and sobbing uncontrollably. Richard put his arms around her shoulders and added his voice to hers as they continued to plead with Raven to get up.

Suddenly, Raven lunged forward and stood up, holding his right foreleg off the ground. Jamie hugged him around the neck and began slowly leading him toward the trailer. He was limping badly, obviously reluctant to put any weight on his injured right foreleg. Richard and the vet leaned carefully under his chest and were relieved to see that the stitches and pressure bandage were holding back the blood.

Raven slowly hobbled up the low ramp into the trailer following the sound of Jan's voice. Jamie got in beside him.

"Jamie, I'm not sure you should try to ride back there with him," warned the Vet. "He may fall over as we move across this bumpy ground and crush you."

"I'll take my chances," Jamie quickly replied. "Just get him to the Vet hospital as quickly as you can."

Richard grabbed some hay and water that Lacey had brought and climbed into the trailer with

Jamie.

"Oh great," moaned the Vet. "Now I have to worry about both of you." He shook his head as Jim jumped into the passenger seat beside him.

"You got a CD player in this rig?" asked Jim.

"Sure, I do," said the Vet. "I listen to Jan's music all the time. Here," he said turning on the truck CD player. "Hear that?" he asked. "That's her latest CD." He slowly pulled away from the campsite and headed carefully across the pasture with Jim sticking his head out the window to warn him of any major bumps and holes. Brett rode ahead of them leading them to the gravel road that ran across his property out to the main highway.

Chapter 29

Brett jumped off the bed and grabbed his ringing cell phone. He glanced at the clock, "My god," he moaned, "it's three o'clock". "Hello," he shouted into the phone.

"Jan's been waking up some," yelled Justin.

"Thank you, God," responded Brett, sinking back down on the bed. "How is she? Does she remember what happened?"

"She's drifting in and out," answered Justin, "so I'm not sure what she remembers. When she saw the gardenias, she knew that you'd been here. Why didn't you wake me up?"

"You just looked so comfortable hanging over that metal rail," teased Brett.

"Yea, right. I have a terrible stiff neck. I can't even turn my head to the right at all."

Brett laughed. "Where are you? Are you still at the hospital?"

"No, I'm on the way home. Mom is staying with her. Jamie, Roger and Beth have stopped in throughout the day. I understand they've got the infection under control with Raven, but Jamie and Richard plan to stay with him until they release him, so they were heading back to the vet hospital."

"That's great news," responded Brett. "I had intended to come over to the hospital as soon as I got cleaned up this morning, but I decided to just lay

213

down across the bed for only a minute or two. I can't believe I slept so long. Anyway, do you think Lacey would mind, if I slipped in to check on Jan for a bit."

"Just do me one favor," said Justin suddenly becoming serious.

"Sure. What?" asked Brett.

"If she wakes up while you're there, don't take off right away."

"Of course not, why would I?"

"Well, that seems to be your style. How many times did you turn your back and ride away from her at the World Show; even today, you ran out."

Brett sat silently staring at the phone.

"You still there?" shouted Justin. "Don't you dare hang up on me, you coward."

"I'm still here, Justin," responded Brett sighing audibly. "I didn't really run away. Jan just shut me down every time I tried to get close to her. I didn't have any choice but to ride off."

"She sees it a whole lot differently," said Justin. "Trust me on this one. See ya," he said snapping his phone shut.

Brett sat down on the side of the bed, staring at his phone. *What did he mean by 'she sees it a whole lot differently'* he wondered. "I asked her out twice, no three times, and she said *no*. What was I supposed to do? Beg for god's sake?" He grabbed his boots and shoved his feet into them. "Brett Kendall has never begged for anything," he shouted as he stormed out of the bedroom.

When he arrived at the hospital, he stopped by the gift shop and picked out another planter with gardenias. Lacey greeted him as he entered Jan's

214

room. "Those are beautiful," she said reaching out to take the flowers from him. "You know how much she loves these. It's very thoughtful. How are you doing with all this?" she asked getting up from the chair next to Jan's bed and motioning for him to sit down.

"Thanks, but you go ahead and sit there," responded Brett walking to the other side of the bed. "I'll just stand. I'm only going to stay a minute."

At the sound of his voice, Jan began to toss her head from side to side and twist around uneasily in the bed. Lacey immediately leaned over to stroke her gently across the forehead. "She must have recognized your voice," she said. "She's called out your name several times since I've been here."

Brett stared at Lacey in disbelief. "M..my name?" he stuttered.

"Several times," Lacey whispered. "I'm glad she's finally found someone she cares about besides that crazy horse. By the way, we sure do appreciate all your help last night. That was ingenious playing Jan's music to get Raven into that trailer this morning."

"Raven.." moaned Jan, fluttering her eyes. "Brett, help Raven," she shouted.

Brett instinctively reached out and gently lifted her hand to his lips. "Raven's doing fine," he whispered softly kissing her pale, small fingers. Jan didn't respond, but she immediately stopped flailing around in the bed.

"She comes and goes like that," consoled Lacey, noting the sadness in Brett's eyes. "The doctor told us that it was normal for someone with such a severe concussion, but it's certainly unnerving."

"If you don't care, I've changed my mind," Brett responded. "I want to stay here for a while." Without letting go of Jan's hand, he reached behind him with his foot and slid a chair up to the side of her bed.

"If you're sure you don't mind staying for the evening, I think I'll head back to the ranch to check on Justin. He's really taking all this pretty hard." She got up and slipped on her jacket. "Are you sure you can stay until someone comes back? I'll send Roger and Beth over as soon as I get home. We don't want to leave her alone."

"I'm not going anywhere this time," said Brett, gently stroking Jan's hand. "Please, don't bother to send anyone back. I promise; I won't leave her alone tonight or ever again," he whispered, holding Jan's fingers against his warm lips.

Lacey smiled at him and patted him on the shoulder. "Love sometimes is messy," she said, as she headed out the door.

After she left, Brett leaned over and let the tears that he had been holding in check all day stream shamelessly down his cheeks. He finally raised his head to look out the large window on the other side of the room at the beautiful Texas sunset. "Keep your eyes on heaven," he whispered. Looking up into the brilliant orange sky he prayed, "Please, dear God, give me another chance with her." When he looked back at Jan, he was shocked when he found himself staring into her sparkling, emerald green eyes.

"Hey, you," she whispered softly, "why the tears?" she asked touching his cheek gently with her hand.

Brett jumped up from his chair, completely startled that she was awake.

"You'd better not be thinking about running away

216

again," she warned reaching her hand out to him.

Brett took hold of her small hand and smiled. He leaned over and gently kissed her soft lips. "This cowboy is never going to ride away from you again. I promise," he said.

****